ONWARD, CRISPY SHOULDERS!
An Extraordinary Life with an Extra Chromosome

by Mary Haakenson Perry

Publication of Wizard Works

Published by
Wizard Works, P.O. Box 1125, Homer, AK 99603

Acknowledgements

I would like to thank my parents, Lionel and Esther Haakenson, and my brothers Tim, Robert, John, Ken, and Ron for sharing their memories to assist me in the writing of this book. Thanks, also, to the many relatives, friends, and working colleagues of Jim who willingly contributed stories. My husband, Charlie, has been a great support and gave excellent suggestions and input. Aurora Firth took my fuzzy pictures and even fuzzier descriptions and created the wonderful picture of Jim on the front cover. Finally, I thank my editor, Jan O'Meara of Wizard Works, whose expertise and encouragement helped me put the whole thing together.

Dedication

This book is dedicated to the memory of my brother, Jim Haakenson.

Prologue

"Hi-yo Silver! Awa-a-a-a-y!" The full-throated cry rings through the quiet spruce forest. Before the echoes die away, a boy appears on a rough, packed-dirt path between the trees, pedaling his bicycle as fast as the rutted surface allows. Bike and rider flash past the solitary log cabin and down another similar, but slightly wider trail, in hot pursuit of an imaginary Bad Guy.

Apparently deciding to continue the chase on foot, the youngster flings himself off the bike. With a shove of the handlebars and an admonition to "Go hide in the bushes, Silver," the fearless hero dashes into the cover of the nearby trees. Silver, an old blue one-speed whose body bears mute testimony to prior experience with similar adventures, wobbles on, riderless, for several feet before collapsing into the fireweed.

Meanwhile, the battle rages on. The young defender of justice crouches for safety behind an uprooted tree stump. Occasionally he ventures out far enough to spray his foe with hot lead from a deadly forefinger. Anyone privileged to witness this drama can keep track of the action by the steady stream of sound effects: "Pow-pow! Get back, Tonto! Pow-pow!"

"Oooh—he got me!" This last, presumably, is from the Bad Guy, since the boy soon emerges from cover, collects Silver, and rides triumphantly back to the house, having rid the world of another dangerous villain.

As the lad draws near, the observer notes that he is a young man in his early teens. His face holds an expression of satisfaction at the battle just won. Also evident are the slightly slanted eyes, the small head and ears, flattened face and larger-than-normal lips and tongue—all unmistakable features of Down's syndrome.

The hero of this story is my oldest brother, Jim. Throughout his life he overcame a myriad of real-life obstacles and even a few "bad guys" who stood in his way. In the process, he lived with a gusto and style that were his very own. As he neared the end of his life, I thought back on all the "Jim stories" that have become a part of our family's memory and the "Jim-isms" (his favorite words and phrases) that continue to flavor our speech.

Beyond those, though, Jim provided an example and inspiration to scores of people with whom he came in contact. I hope his story will encourage you, as well.

Early Delivery

May 1945. It was springtime in Alaska, the season when the sun shines warmly and soft winds gently sway the newly-budded branches of the birch trees. But this was Atka, a remote island of the Aleutian Chain. A place only the Army could love. Or so it seemed to its current residents, a few dozen men who wore the uniforms of the United States armed forces. (The military loved it so much, in fact, that they relocated the island's original residents—a small, hardy band of Aleuts—to another part of Alaska, thus allowing the army to have the whole island to themselves for the duration of the war.)

On Atka there were no trees, budding or otherwise. The sun probably shone somewhere, but it rarely made an appearance through the mist and fog shrouding the island. There was, however, wind, its intensity rivaled only by the intensity with which the servicemen daily calculated—to the minute — their remaining tenure on this barren rock.

My father, Lionel Haakenson, was one of these soldiers. A transplanted North Dakota farm boy, he moved to Alaska in 1937 to make his fortune prospecting for gold. That didn't work out, but he stayed on in the Matanuska Valley, an area known for its fertile land some fifty miles north of Anchorage. The government's Matanuska Colonization Program had brought 200 families from Minnesota, Wisconsin and Michigan in 1935 and '36. The project aimed to give these Midwest farm families—hard-hit by the Depression—a new start in life, farming the valley's rich soil. As a strong kid who understood farming and wasn't afraid of hard work, Lionel easily found a variety of jobs with the colonists and people he met in Anchorage.

On one of his jobs, Lionel met Esther Larson, the daughter of a colonist family. Their friendship grew over the course of several years, leading them to the brink of engagement. Then the attack on Pearl Harbor in 1941 impelled Lionel to join the Army Air Corps. As Alaska was considered (and subsequently proven) vulnerable to attack, not surprisingly, Lionel's duty assignment stationed him in his adopted state.

He told the recruiters he wanted to be a pilot, but they apparently thought at twenty-seven he was too old for such dangerous duty. Upon interviewing him, they discovered that, just prior to joining, he'd been working for an electrical contractor. They decided such experience qualified him to become a telephone and electrical maintenance man. He spent a year at Elmendorf Air Force Base in Anchorage learning the necessary skills for that job, as well as perfecting the essential military requirements of saluting and marching. During this interlude he presented Esther with a ring. They agreed to marry as soon as the war was over.

Just before Thanksgiving, 1942, Lionel shipped out for Atka. There, he and his comrades were charged with maintenance of a small airstrip which had been constructed for use by military planes. For the most part, the troops on Atka received little attention, the pilots preferring to land at larger bases such as Adak or Shemya.

Lionel remained on Atka, except for brief furloughs taken at the army's discretion, for 857 days. (Finally giving up on allowing the length of the war to determine the length of their engagement, he and Esther married during a leave he took at Christmas of 1943.)

Day number 853, on a typical Atka evening, Lionel relaxed in the quiet darkness of the mess hall where the weekly movie was being shown. It didn't really matter what the movie was; at least it was indoors, out of the wind. Lionel paid less than usual attention to the screen. He thought about Esther back in Anchorage. Now, with the war almost over and military operations winding down, he was going home to live in the same place as his wife. Thanks to a short furlough last fall, when he'd gotten to spend some time in Anchorage, there was a baby on the way, and he'd be home in time for the birth. Although he'd be happy either way, he kind of hoped for a boy. He'd always wanted a little boy called Jimmy. His mind wandered off on another path. He imagined himself teaching Jimmy to ride a bike, taking him to his first day of school, watching him grow into a handsome, successful adult…

Suddenly a voice boomed through the quiet of the theater: "Telegram for Sergeant Haakenson!" Lionel jumped in surprise, then quickly slipped out of the room. Telegrams meant really good news, or really bad news. People didn't send telegrams just to say hello. He snatched up the small yellow envelope and tore it open. With growing astonishment and elation, he read the simple message:

ANCHORAGE ALASKA MAY 9 1945 DEAREST LIONEL
JAMES LIONEL ARRIVED AT THREE FORTY THIS
MORNING HE WEIGHED FIVE POUNDS FIFTEEN AND
ONE HALF OUNCES WE ARE BOTH DOING FINE BUT
HOPE YOU CAN COME SOON ... ALL OUR LOVE
FOREVER   ESTHER HAAKENSON

The message contained a few more details dealing with
other family matters, but Lionel barely noticed that part. A son!
He was a daddy! He thankfully noted that both were well,
though he had no reason to expect otherwise. He joyfully began
packing his belongings, anxious to leave this desolate island
and rejoin his wife and new son in Anchorage. What slipped
his mind was his wife's penchant for understatement. He
wouldn't know until he arrived back home that his son's entrance into the world was not as uncomplicated as the telegram
implied.

Esther had awakened on the morning of May 8; her water
had just broken. Apparently, this baby—not due for another
three weeks—was in a hurry to arrive. Now what? She couldn't
call her husband to help; he was more than fourteen hundred
miles away, on Atka. Besides, a phone remained something of a
luxury item in this outpost of civilization, a luxury Esther
didn't possess. She sent up a small prayer of thanks that the
snow banks that lined the streets a week or so ago had mostly
melted. She had enough things to worry about without the
added headache of slick streets.

"Well, Esther," she murmured, "It looks like you're about
to have a baby, ready or not. Lying here isn't going to help;
you'd better get a move on."

She got up and dressed with care, determined not to
present herself to the medical staff with her hair un-
combed or her clothes wrinkled. She slipped into one of
her few maternity dresses. In spite of her advanced preg-
nancy and petite, 5' 4" frame, she had, until recently, been
able to continue wearing her regular clothes. Most people
had no idea she was so near her due date.

Satisfied that her hair and clothes were presentable, she tidied
up the two-room house; after all, there might be well-meaning friends
coming by to help out when she brought the baby home. She
couldn't have them thinking she was a messy housekeeper.

She couldn't resist one last inspection of the project that had kept her busy all winter: a homemade baby crib. Lumber was in short supply due to the war, and a new, store-bought crib was beyond her budget. Such considerations barely caused Esther to blink. Gathering what scraps of lumber she could find, she ripped them with a hand saw to the appropriate widths. All through the cold, dark winter she measured, sawed, drilled and hammered. Once she finished the frame, she sewed a mattress and added sheets and blankets. Now the bed stood ready for its tiny occupant. Giving the covers a final tug and pat, she ran a critical eye around the room. Satisfied that everything was in order, she ran down the street to her neighbor, who dropped everything and rushed her to the hospital.

By midnight Esther suspected the early morning trip to the hospital might have been a little precipitous. The baby was coming, but was taking its time. The hours crept by as she lay in the labor room. The nurses looked in on her occasionally. She dreamt about the baby: would it be a boy or a girl? Wouldn't Lionel be surprised to find out he was a father several weeks early!

Finally, about three o'clock the next morning, the baby decided that the time was right. The team assembled, and in another 40 minutes, Esther gave birth to a son. Now she could relax. The hard part was over. Or was it? Weren't babies supposed to cry when they're born? Wasn't that the way they took their first breath? Why wasn't her baby crying? And why were all the doctors and nurses working over him so intently?

Suddenly she heard the doctor snap, "Get the oxygen in here–now!" A nurse dashed from the room and returned with a cart carrying the oxygen machine. As the doctor reached for the cart, Esther caught a glimpse of the infant; his face was blue. This couldn't be happening to her brand-new son. "Oh, breathe, Jimmy, *breathe!*" Agonizing seconds passed before she heard the sound she'd been praying for. A weak, quavering wail signaled that the baby's lungs had begun functioning.

Soon a relieved nurse handed the now-squalling infant to Esther. She comforted him until he quieted, then she closely inspected the tiny person, counting fingers and toes, marveling at the perfection of his form. Without a doubt, she knew he was the most beautiful and perfect baby ever to make an entrance into the world.

Some twenty months later, Esther eyed her grinning firstborn with an expression in which fondness battled with frustration. *Why won't Jimmy walk?* She watched him, standing in the middle of the living room, acting so proud of himself. If he didn't get moving, his brother Timmy–his junior by ten months–would be walking before he was. She moved closer and extended a finger. Jimmy grasped it and toddled along beside her. Quickly she pulled the finger away; Jimmy stopped.

"It's always this way," she related in a conversation with her sister Gladys. "He'll walk holding a finger or someone's pant leg, but take the support away and he just stands. And stands. And stands."

The two sat and watched Gladys' two boys as they played with Jimmy and Timmy, mentally comparing Jimmy's developmental milestones with those of his cousins. Obviously, Jimmy was rapidly losing ground, but why? Thinking about her mother's last visit from the Matanuska farm, Esther spoke again, "Mom mentioned it when she saw the kids. I told her the doctor said he was fine, but I don't think she believes it. I know something's wrong, but what?" Gladys shook her head, as mystified as Esther.

"You're going to have to start getting around under your own steam," she told him now. "You're almost a year and a half old; you and Timmy are getting too heavy to carry." Jimmy beamed at her.

Esther thought back over the months since she and Jimmy came home from the hospital. The words of the woman in charge of the nursery still rang in her ears: "Don't let him be lazy. You've got to make him nurse." At the time, Esther thought the nurse was just showing solicitude for a mother with her first baby: "He sleeps too much...He eats too little...He's not as alert as he should be...Talk to him more...feed him more...play with him more."

Esther hadn't been overly concerned, thinking the woman knew nothing of the trauma Jimmy had endured just to make it into the world. "Maybe," she thought, "that nurse wouldn't feel so frisky herself if she'd been the one who turned blue."

Now she conceded that the nurse had known what she was talking about. For some reason, Jimmy was proving to be a slow learner. Although a happy, affectionate little boy, he seemed uninterested in learning anything new. Aside from potty-training (which he learned within two days at the age of one), everything else he had learned—sitting up, feeding himself with a spoon, even responding to his name—came about only through many repetitions and much patient teaching. Of course, on the plus side, once he learned something, he never forgot it. Take eating, for example: yes, he was slow to begin nursing, but once over that hurdle, no one feared that Jimmy would starve—he loved food.

As she watched him, she wondered again which family member he resembled. She and Lionel had studied his round face, the curiously slanted eyes, the small nose. Aside from his light hair and blue eyes, he bore little resemblance to either parent or any relative that they could think of. She often sensed that he had trouble with his tongue, as if it were too large for his mouth. Even his short, stubby body and short, broad hands and fingers didn't fit into the typical Haakenson/Larson mold. They figured he must be a throwback to some unknown ancestor.

Back to the walking problem. There comes a time in every mother's life when she must scrap the honest, direct approach. Esther reluctantly admitted to herself that she had reached this point. It was time to take it to the next level: bribery, embellished with just a touch of trickery:

Jimmy stands where Mamma has placed him, his back against the couch. He can feel the support behind him, but can't grab hold of anything. What is Mamma up to? She's in front of him now, with a cookie in her hand; she knows how to capture his attention. Crouching down, she waves that cookie and coaxes him in her most persuasive voice.

"Look, Jimmy, you want a cookie? Come here and get it."

Jimmy eyes the cookie. He can almost taste it. If he stretches out just a little further...the cookie moves! What is Mamma thinking? He gazes at her, slightly offended, then makes a quick grab. Again he comes up with nothing. He leans away from the couch. He's so close. His hand takes another swipe at the cookie. At the same time his foot, which had been firmly planted in front of the couch, comes off the floor. A pudgy leg follows the direction of the reaching arm. Then the other foot comes forward. And the prize is his! He doesn't know why Mamma is acting so strangely. She's bouncing up and down till she's almost coming off the floor. She must be glad he got the cookie. He smiles up at Mamma and munches his prize.

Thus another obstacle in Jimmy's life was overcome. He could walk, although he would suffer many falls and bruises before becoming proficient. But the mystery remained: why did it take so long for him to learn each new skill?

Esther broached the subject each time she brought the boys in for their checkups, but the doctor dismissed her fears. He checked Jimmy's reflexes with his little rubber mallet, looked into his ears, listened to his heart, and pronounced, "He's fine; babies just develop at different rates." Thus reassured, my parents continued enjoying their young son, teaching him when he appeared ready to learn, just loving him the rest of the time.

The Answer

Esther's sister Gladys gazed at Jimmy, worry clouding her face. She had been baby-sitting him and Timmy daily during the last days of January 1948, while Esther spent the requisite week in the hospital following the birth of her third child.

Gladys looked over at Timmy, laughing and tumbling around the floor with her three youngsters. He seemed content to spend his days with his cousins, confident that he would see his mother when she got out of the hospital. Each morning when Lionel dropped him and Jimmy off on his way to work, he dived right into a game, showing no sign of being upset by Esther's absence.

Jimmy was a different matter entirely. He huddled on a little stool, his body sagging, the very picture of misery. Timmy and the cousins occasionally invited him to play, or came over to offer him a toy, but he remained wrapped in his sadness. All week, every morning, he plopped onto the stool, and there he stayed. His eyes, full of his inner pain, stared dully into space. His mouth sagged open slightly, as if closing it took too much effort. Gladys wished he would cry or ask to sit on her lap—anything—so she could comfort him.

"He acts like this at home, too. I'm even having trouble getting him to eat anything." Lionel's concerned words echoed in Gladys' mind.

Grimly she muttered to herself, "I'm glad Esther's coming home today, before the poor child literally dies of grief or starves to death."

Dropping to her knees, she slowly crept up behind Jimmy's chair. This was a favorite game they had played since he was an infant. Popping her head up next to him, she sang out, "Peek-a-boo!" No response. Auntie may look and even sound a lot like Mamma, but she was not Mamma.

Just then, a commotion at the door attracted her attention. "Thank God," she thought, scrambling up from her knees, "Esther and the baby are here." She hurried to help Esther with baby Robert, coat, boots, and diaper bag. Timmy and the cousins also ran over to greet her and examine the new baby. Jimmy remained slumped on the stool, oblivious to the activity in the room.

Gladys, seeing that Esther was anxious to go to Jimmy,

took little Bobby and sat down so the other kids could inspect him. Esther approached the forlorn little figure on the stool. "Jimmy," she called gently, "Mamma's here."

Slowly Jimmy turned toward her voice. His eyes focused on the face he apparently thought he would never see again. "Mamma," he said wonderingly.

Light and life returned to his eyes. Esther picked him up, and he clung to her as if he would never let go. The first smile anyone had seen from him in a week split his face from ear to ear. Mamma was back; all was well with his world.

On a cold February day shortly after Bobby's arrival, Lionel and Esther unexpectedly received an answer to their questions about Jimmy. In the doctor's waiting room, Lionel tossed aside a magazine and looked over at Jimmy and Timmy, quietly amusing themselves with a handkerchief. Jimmy, now two and a half, draped the handkerchief over his head, so it hung down in front of his eyes. He chuckled delightedly as Timmy playfully snatched the hanky away. Jimmy made a grab for it and Timmy tossed it back onto Jimmy's head. They both giggled.

"Mr. and Mrs. Haakenson? The doctor will see you now." The young nurse smiled as Lionel took Jimmy and Timmy each by a hand and led them into the doctor's office. Esther followed, carrying Bobby. The patients on this visit were Lionel, who spent the week following Esther and Bobby's homecoming in the hospital with a serious strep infection, and Bobby, who was in for his first checkup. Lionel settled the two older boys side by side in chairs, where they sat quietly, continuing to play with the handkerchief. The family doctor began his examination of the baby.

A second doctor, the one who had treated Lionel in the hospital, came in to check on Lionel. Seeing Jimmy, he did a double-take and asked the family doctor, "Is he a Cretin?"

"No, probably a mongoloid," responded the family doctor.

Gesturing toward my parents the other doctor muttered, "Do they know?"

"Oh...yeah," came the reply.

Lionel was too stunned to speak. How long had Esther known about this? Why on earth hadn't she told him? He directed an accusing look at her, only to see a similar expression on her face. She didn't know either! The rest of the visit passed as if in the blurred unreality of a nightmare. Finally, gathering up their boys, they left the doctor's office.

As they stepped out into the briskness of the winter day, the shock of chilly air was nothing compared with the shock of the doctor's words. "What did they call Jimmy? Cretin? Mongoloid? I've never heard those words." Lionel still couldn't believe what he'd heard.

"I remember hearing the terms in school," said Esther uncertainly. "I think they have something to do with how much a person can learn. Where did I put that medical book? I'm going to look them up."

At home, Esther hunted up the medical encyclopedia while Lionel grabbed his favorite reference–the dictionary. They found the terms "cretin" and "Mongoloid," and read to each other the few lines of information provided by these sources. The encyclopedia (which, to spare its makers embarrassment, shall remain anonymous) contained a description of mongolism which was more complete, but still daunting:

Mongolism is a peculiar condition of unknown cause. It is not hereditary. It shows itself soon after birth and is characterized by slanting eyes, broad nose, small head, loose joints, large hands and feet, protruding abdomen, idiocy, and often congenital heart disease and other physical defects. Such infants, fortunately, usually die soon after birth, but occasionally one lives to become an adult. There is no cure for the condition, and no useful treatment.

It was hard to apply the impersonal words to Jimmy. Some of the characteristics fit, some didn't. But there were enough similarities to convince them: Jimmy was a Mongoloid.

Although they were shocked by the doctor's lack of candor—especially in view of the number of times the subject had been raised—my parents did not regard the information as life-shattering. They actually felt relief knowing the reason why Jimmy was so slow.

I have often wondered if the doctor also felt relieved that the difficult chore of telling my parents was over with so little fuss. Not being the type to make a scene, they had left without saying much of anything, so he probably felt that he escaped pretty easily. Possibly he felt inadequate to provide information, when so little was known about the condition.

Those few stark statements, with no personal comments to soften their impact, remained my parents' only official information about Down's syndrome for several decades.

Seattle Visit

Down's syndrome—what used to be known as Mongolism—is a baffling condition, principally because it appears seemingly at random. It happens as cells divide in the early stages of fetal development. When, for unknown reasons, a cell divides unevenly, the developing child picks up an extra chromosome. We know that older mothers with older eggs are at greater risk for a child with Down's syndrome (DS), but a large number of young mothers, in prime childbearing years, also give birth to children with the condition. The best explanation I have heard for the occurrence is that it is an accident of nature. Nothing the parent does will cause or prevent it, and, except for the relatively rare cases in which there is a family history of more than one child with DS, it usually strikes once and does not reappear within a given family.

Adding that one little extra chromosome to each cell affects every aspect of the person. Many have malformed hearts or other internal organs. Even those who escape major medical problems have a number of characteristics which we associate with DS. (These characteristics often cause those with the disorder to look more like each other than they do members of their own families.) Though the characteristics vary from person to person, the majority have overall low muscle tone. This affects every body movement from walking, to hand grasp (affecting such movements as writing or picking up small objects,) to posture (they have a more difficult time fighting against the pull of gravity.)

The facial features are the most visible. The eyes are slightly slanted, the face itself is slightly flattened, the lips may be overly large, and the tongue often seems too large for the smaller than normal mouth cavity. As this is uncomfortable, the person may let his or her mouth hang open, or even protrude the tongue slightly. The lips, tongue and other muscles involved in speech production usually have impaired movement, which, along with the large tongue, make clear articulation difficult.

Some level of mental retardation usually accompanies Down's syndrome. Though some people with DS have severe mental impairments, others have the ability to reach a fairly high level of academic achievement. A few have normal or near-normal abilities. All have the capacity to learn, when taught with patience and perseverance. Unfortunately, many people with DS, particularly those of my brother's generation, were not afforded the opportunity to reach their potential. This was often the result of preconceived notions of their abilities, or lack of support and information to help the family and individual with DS discover their strengths.

Despite all these drawbacks, those with DS possess a number of gifts that make them delightful human beings. They can learn, just as other children must, the basics of manners, work ethic, and good citizenship; in fact, these concepts seem to come easier for those with DS. In general, they are highly social, making friends easily and spreading joy wherever they go. They are affectionate and good-natured, kindhearted and generous. They may take a little extra time to learn, but once they grasp a concept, they tend to remember it. Once trained in a job, they take pride in carrying out their tasks precisely as they have been taught.

All this information came to our family long after the arrival of my brother. If we had known all of it from the beginning, what difference would it have made in his life, and the lives of his family members? Would my parents have handled him differently, expected more, expected less? We'll never know for sure. The short answer is, some things may have changed, presumably for the better. The long answer is...well, that's what this book is all about.

Once my parents finally had an explanation, imperfect as it was, they wasted little time with hand-wringing and moans of "Why us?" Instead, they set forth with renewed determination to help Jimmy succeed to the greatest degree possible. They knew he could learn, because they had already taught him many things. With the diagnosis finally out in the open, the doctor felt more inclined to discuss possible treatments for Jimmy. Unfortunately, information about the condition continued to be most remarkable for its scarcity.

Esther questioned the doctor on her next visit: "Several people have told me about thyroid medication being used for people who are slow. Do you think it might help Jimmy?"

"It's worth a try," said the doctor, regardless of what he may have thought privately concerning the efficacy of such treatment. He wrote a prescription, then instructed, "Bring him in for monthly checkups."

Esther faithfully bundled up her three boys and navigated the snowy streets to keep each appointment. This, in itself, was no small feat. First, she faced the challenge of finding a ride. Lionel drove their only car to work, and her sister Gladys had her hands full with her own small children. When Gladys could help, Esther only had to get the boys ready once. If she used their own car, the bundling process happened twice–early, when she took Lionel to work, and again for the drive to the doctor's office.

There, she and the boys could count on spending most of the remainder of the day in the waiting room. When they were finally admitted to the inner sanctum, the doctor examined Jimmy but said little, so Esther didn't know whether or not he saw any improvement from the thyroid pills. She and Lionel did not see any perceptible difference in Jimmy's rate of development.

A few months later, the family doctor died when his private plane crashed. My parents began seeing a new doctor who appeared unimpressed with the thyroid treatment. It seemed like a good time to try a new direction.

"We're planning a trip Outside this fall," Esther informed the doctor. ("Outside" is a generic Alaskan term applied to any state other than Alaska.) "Lionel's family is having a reunion in North Dakota, but we're visiting some relatives in the Seattle area as well. Would it be useful to have a pediatrician out there look at Jimmy?"

The doctor said he thought that sounded like a good idea, apparently feeling out of his depth. As a small-town general practitioner, possibly he thought a pediatrician from a metropolitan area possessed more experience in dealing with children like Jimmy. Or perhaps he thought a stranger was a better candidate to give this family the final word on a long-term prognosis.

Accordingly, August found the family on board a plane heading for their reunion in North Dakota. Here, three-year-old Jimmy made the acquaintance of many of his Haakenson relatives. One who was especially drawn to him was Lionel's older sister, Lillian. She and Jimmy spent many hours together, creating a bond that would endure throughout their lives.

What relatives the family missed while in the Midwest, they met when they reached Seattle. Here Lionel and Esther (thankful indeed for Lionel's large and far-flung family of siblings) found lodging with Lionel's brother Earl. Despite their enjoyment of the time spent visiting and reconnecting with family, they felt an undercurrent of nervousness as they anticipated the upcoming visit to the unknown pediatrician. What would he say? What pronouncements would he make that might affect Jimmy's future?

On the day of the appointment, Earl's wife, Elinor, dropped Esther and Jimmy off at the pediatrician's office on her way to work. (Lionel, designated baby sitter for the day, remained at Earl's with Timmy and Bobby.)

A youngish-looking man in a tan jacket approached the two. "Mrs. Haakenson? Nice to meet you. And this is Jimmy? Come in and let's chat for a while."

Mother and child followed the doctor into the office, where the doctor asked questions and took down information. As the adults talked, Jimmy clung to Esther for a time, then began quietly exploring the room.

"What I'd like to do," said the pediatrician, "is to keep Jimmy with me for the day, take him with me on my rounds, see what he can do, how he interacts with people, toys, his surroundings."

Esther, nervous about leaving her little boy with the doctor, nevertheless knew the two needed time to get acquainted if he was going to be able to make suggestions that would help Jimmy. She was shown to a waiting room and invited to make herself comfortable. There she browsed through a stack of ancient magazines, studied the pictures on the walls and memorized the pattern on the tile floor. Most of all, she waited.

The afternoon was nearly gone before the man brought Jimmy back. Esther greeted them with relief and anticipation, hoping Jimmy had behaved as he had been taught. What kinds of helpful insights would this doctor offer? Surely he, being a specialist in children's medicine, possessed a good bit of experience with children with disabilities. She waited expectantly for his verdict.

The doctor studied his notes. "I have to say," he began, "Jimmy impressed me. You folks deserve a lot of credit for the work you've done. You obviously put a lot of time and effort into teaching him. He's toilet-trained, he's well-mannered and sociable. His table manners are better than many 'normal' kids I know!"

Here he shuffled through his notes, as if to give himself time to choose exactly the right words. Taking a deep breath he continued, "Honestly, though, it would be unfair to your family to keep Jimmy at home. You'll end up wasting all your time and money looking for a 'cure' for his condition. There isn't one. He will never be able to learn; it's very likely he won't live past the age of eighteen. There are several institutions I can recommend. I know a number of the best families in Seattle who have had children like Jimmy. They've put them into one of these centers where they can be with others like themselves. If you keep him at home, it will be a detriment to the whole family—especially any siblings he might have. My advice to you is, put him into one of these institutions and forget you ever had him. Go home, have a couple more babies, and move on with your lives."

Esther felt as if the guy had punched her in the stomach. She and Lionel had been so hopeful that this "expert" could give them some pointers on raising and teaching Jimmy. The man was talking about their son as if he were nothing but an old rag to be disposed of. An institution! She remembered Jimmy's reaction during the week she spent in the hospital when Bobby arrived. She knew he wouldn't last a month if he were taken away from his family.

Despite her intense disappointment and shock, she managed to find her voice: "I already have two more babies, and they aren't suffering at all because of Jimmy. He's part of our family, and we're *not* putting him in an institution!"

Pajama Lessons

The family returned to Anchorage, now aware of what at least part of the medical community advised for Jimmy, but knowing that solution was unacceptable. Jimmy learned things, in his own time. Lionel and Esther, certain about past successes, knew they could do a much better job of raising Jimmy than some impersonal institution. For lack of any better ideas or direction, they continued treating him as much like the other boys as possible.

"Take the arms and fold them this way. Now fold it in half like this." Esther guided Jimmy's small hands through the process of folding his pajamas. Timmy and little Bobby watched carefully, then copied the moves with their own pajamas.

Esther liked a tidy house and, with the arrival of little Johnny, less than a year after the trip Outside, acknowledged that she needed help. She knew the only way to maintain order was to assign chores to everyone capable of performing them. The first lesson, she decided, would be to teach the boys how to care for their own nightclothes. She expected as much from Jimmy as the other boys, although she made allowances in the amount of assistance and the length of teaching time needed.

"Now the bottoms." Again she assisted as Jimmy fumbled with the material. His fingers would not do what he wanted them to. Esther persisted; she knew that, with time, he would master the task.

"When they're folded, I want you to put them in here." She led the boys to a small chest with three drawers, one for each of them. Jimmy opened his drawer and she showed him exactly where the pajamas should go. Timmy and Bobby followed suit.

In this task, Jimmy had a hidden advantage over his brothers. Through the years most of Esther's children proved not to have inherited her neatness gene. Jimmy had it in spades. Once he understood and mastered the task of folding those pajamas, he faithfully folded and tucked them into the designated corner of that drawer. When wash day came the other boys' garments may have been strewn around, but Jimmy's, never.

If there was a positive side to the doctor's reticence in revealing Jim's condition, it was that it gave my parents time to discover Jim's abilities. Had they known his condition at his birth, they might not have had the same expectations or persevered so doggedly in their teaching. As it was, they knew that, given time and persistent teaching, Jim learned things very well. Throughout his life, the rewards for teaching such simple tasks as the pajama lessons continued. He always neatly put away his clothes, made his bed, and stowed his possessions in their appointed places.

With several small boys of similar size, Esther faced another challenge in her never-ending quest for order and organization. She solved the problem of identifying whose pants were whose by embroidering their first names in block letters on the waistbands, each boy's in a different color. Even at their tender ages Jimmy, Timmy and Bobby quickly became proficient at spotting their names. In Jimmy's case, he would proudly hold his pants up and state, "That's my J." So a simple solution to a housekeeping issue turned into a meaningful reading readiness exercise.

With no professional guidance, my parents relied on instinct and common sense. They continued to raise Jimmy in the way that seemed best to them, keeping a positive view of his abilities and their role in his continued progress. This attitude surfaced one day as Esther visited with a friend who also had a child with a handicap. The woman confided, "I try to figure out what I did, why God is punishing me by giving me this child. Do you ever think about that?"

Surprised, Esther replied, "I don't think God is punishing us. I believe He chose us as Jimmy's parents because He knew we were the best ones for the job. It's up to us to live up to His expectations and make Jimmy's life the best we can."

Jimmy displayed this same kind of faith in God's wisdom and goodness:

"Jesus loves me, this I know; for the Bible tells me so." The words of the familiar song issued enthusiastically if inexpertly from the throats of the small group of Sunday School participants. Jimmy's eyes gleamed with pleasure. He loved singing. His mouth and tongue wouldn't cooperate for him to pronounce most of the words, but he joined in on the chorus anyway, "Na, na-na-na ME-E-E-E-E!" His voice boomed out on the final word of the phrase, a beat or two behind the rest of the group, "Na, na-na-na ME." The teacher smiled at him as the group finished the song, "Yes, Jesus loves me, the Bible tells me so."

The next song was "Wide, Wide as the Ocean." Jimmy jigged up and down in his chair; this was one of his favorites—it had motions! He stretched his arms wide like the other kids, reached high, then low.

He was proud of knowing the words, even though he couldn't say them very well. He got lots of practice; in addition to attending Sunday School each week, Mamma found some time almost every day to sing with him and his brothers. A lady from the church also visited their home each week and conducted a time of singing and Bible stories for the neighborhood kids. In the summer came a special treat—Daily Vacation Bible School. A whole week–sometimes two–of going to church every day. Jimmy felt as if he were enjoying a taste of Heaven here on earth. If he had his way, he'd make church a daily occurrence all year long.

Thanks to all these experiences, Jimmy learned at a young age how to behave in class and other public places. He was content to sit and listen quietly during lessons and sermons, even though much of them escaped his comprehension. He did not concern himself with things that were too deep for him. The song said Jesus loved him, and that was good enough for him.

Driving the Alcan

The big blue Pontiac sedan bumped slowly down the Alcan Highway. Even at this pace, the car sent up an immense cloud of dust, obscuring from view any sights worth seeing.

Lionel peered into the rear view mirror. "You boys better straighten up, or we'll have to stop and have a 'discussion' about how to behave in the car." Three little boys in the back seat straightened up... temporarily, at least. Jimmy warily watched his brothers from a safe distance–as distant as he could manage in a back seat containing four squirming youngsters; then, leaning his head back against the seat, he drifted off to sleep.

Two-year-old Johnny, already showing signs of becoming an imp, moved his foot closer to his three-year-old brother's. If he can get it to...just...barely...touch...

"Mamma!" yelled Bobby, "Johnny touched my foot!"

Timmy waded in to referee. Bobby naturally took exception to this high-handed behavior from someone only two years his senior, and the back seat again erupted in fraternal warfare.

Lionel may no longer have served in the military, but he could still summon up his sergeant's voice when the occasion demanded. "Boys! Do I need to stop this car?"

 The message sank in this time, and the combatants subsided. Daddy's words brought back the memory of yesterday's showdown, when he actually did stop the car. Not only did he stop it, but he made the boys get out—right there in the middle of nowhere—and he LEFT! (In reality, he let the car roll slowly forward about ten feet, but they felt like they had run miles before he let them back in the car.) They weren't going to chance a repeat of that particular experience, so they contented themselves with fearsome but wordless glowering.

"Now look what you've done," scolded Esther. "You woke up Mary!" At five months old, I was the newest member of the family. Esther had just lulled me to sleep on the front seat between herself and Lionel. Now I was wide awake and screaming; not only did I hate traveling, but the interrupted nap stoked my fury. On top of that, I was on the verge of breaking out with chicken pox, though my folks wouldn't find that out for several more days.

What would have brought an otherwise sane family to attempt such a trip? Seventeen hundred miles of gravel road are no picnic under the best of conditions, and these were barely passable. The new Alaska-Canada Highway (better known as the Alcan) had not yet had time to prove its worth as a route for civilian traffic. The military punched it through in 1942 and '43 to move supplies into Alaska for the war effort. Crews worked quickly, giving little thought to comfort and convenience.

Spanning the distance from Fairbanks, Alaska, to Dawson Creek in British Columbia, the road covers an area of the globe not known for its hospitable landscape. Temperatures along the route range from over 90 degrees Fahrenheit in the summer to minus 50 degrees, or lower, in the winter. This sort of temperature fluctuation can wreak havoc on a road, causing spectacular humps and dips as the frost comes and goes with the seasons. Factor in the added thrills of narrow mountain roads with switchbacks, hairpin curves, and dizzyingly deep valleys mere inches from the car, and our trip became a sort of week-long, thirty-mile-an-hour roller-coaster ride.

On sunny days the dust, in addition to obscuring all vision, settled into noses, throats, hair, and clothing. Rains turned the road into a muddy, slippery quagmire. More than once the car had gotten stuck. This was not a drive to be undertaken lightly, especially in a car containing five small children. What seemed like a great adventure a week ago was now just a long, dusty road. The children were hot, bored, and cranky. So were the parents.

As they bounced along, Esther and Lionel tried to push their present discomfort aside and focus on the purpose of the trip. Their destination was California, where they hoped to find a school for Jimmy.

The odyssey actually began more than a year earlier, when my parents started looking into the possibility of obtaining the special help Jimmy needed to attend school. He had turned five in May of 1950, so should have been eligible for kindergarten in the fall. They knew that, though well-behaved and competent with basic self-help skills, he would not be able to keep up in a regular classroom. Due to diminished ability to control the muscles of his mouth and lips and a tongue thickened as a result of Down's syndrome, his speech was slurred and difficult to understand. Also, despite my parents' efforts to teach him, he lacked the pre-academic requirements of the public school system.

By the fall of 1950, Lionel and Esther had exhausted every lead they could find in the Anchorage vicinity. The public schools had no programs for children with special needs, and refused to consider Jimmy as a student. The few private schools in the Anchorage area cost more money than the family could afford. My parents grew increasingly frustrated as they saw the school year beginning, but no openings for him. They knew that Jimmy could learn; he just required a program designed around his needs.

As they began to despair of ever finding a school for him, Lionel's sister Lillian, Jimmy's boon companion from the North Dakota reunion, brought forward an idea. Lil, who lived in Los Angeles, sent a magazine article about a boarding school in her area. Specially geared to educate those with retardation, it offered as an extra benefit administration of a supplement known as glutamic acid. Many considered it a miracle cure, capable of increasing the intellectual ability of those who took it. Lionel and Esther, though still unwilling to make such a huge step, felt they had to give the matter some consideration.

Letters flew back and forth between Aunt Lil and my parents over the next months. Lil checked out the school and came away impressed. It was close to her home, and she expressed her willingness to pick Jimmy up on Friday evenings, keep him through the weekends, and drive him back on Monday mornings. During the week, he would live at the school in a cottage with a house mother and three other young students. Though they hated the idea of sending Jimmy so far from home, my parents eventually conceded it seemed to be their only alternative. At least he would enjoy a regular family contact with an aunt who, though childless herself, loved him as if he were her own.

So began our family's trek across a large portion of North America. After again taking a big loop eastward for family visits in North Dakota and Minnesota, we arrived, weary and sick of traveling, in Los Angeles at Aunt Lillian's. She and her husband Cliff extended a warm welcome. Certain that this would solve Jimmy's schooling difficulties, they couldn't wait to introduce the school to Jimmy and my parents.

As the car pulled up at the school, my parents viewed it

with a mixture of hope and doubt. Hope, because from what they had read and heard, this school sounded like the sort of place that could help Jimmy. Doubt, because they had learned, in the six short years of his life, that not everyone shared their expectations or belief in Jimmy's potential.

Even from the outside, the place looked promising. A large fenced yard contained lots of playground equipment; they knew Jimmy would enjoy that. A big old house had been remodeled into a number of boarding rooms, each containing a house parent and several students.

Once inside the school they felt their doubts receding. Jimmy's prospective house parent, Mrs. Von Aspern was a warm, motherly woman; Jimmy responded to her immediately. The children all seemed happy and well cared for. Some, obviously with Down's syndrome, had features strikingly similar to Jimmy's. All the students crowded around the visitors with right hands outstretched–they all wanted to shake hands. Obviously, someone had taught them proper etiquette when being introduced to strangers.

After several visits to the school, and with Lil's urging, Lionel and Esther agreed to enroll Jimmy for one year. The tuition costs would have been difficult to meet for an extended period, but for the time being they had funds at their disposal. During the past year Lionel had built a house for a middle-aged couple in Anchorage. The buyers gave my parents the Pontiac as a down payment, and the monthly payments would just cover the cost of Jimmy's tuition. The Lord truly works in marvelous ways.

All too soon the day arrived when my parents knew they could no longer delay their departure. They needed to head north and get home before winter settled over those hundreds of Alcan miles. They could see that Jimmy's visits to the school had made him feel quite at home. They explained that he would be staying there to go to school. Though he didn't under-stand all that entailed, he'd heard them say the magic word: school. Through his experiences with Sunday School he knew a little about school–enough to know that he loved it.

My parents also drew comfort from watching the renewed friendship between Jimmy and Aunt Lil. Knowing he was going to get to spend lots of time with his Auntie Lil was another plus, as far as Jimmy was concerned. It was obvious to all that the two were delighted with each other. As hard as this separation would be on the family, it would have been impossible were Lil not there to watch over him.

Lionel and Esther agonized over the best way to handle the parting. Esther's absences during the births of Johnny and me hadn't brought on the kind of trauma witnessed during that terrible week when Bobby was born; still, Jimmy's world revolved around his family. How would he react to the sudden disappearance of Daddy, Mamma, his brothers and sister? Would he pine away and die as he almost had once before? Or would Lil's presence and school be sufficient distraction to keep him occupied until he adjusted?

In the end, my parents decided against a long, emotional farewell, feeling it might only upset Jimmy and delay his settling-in. So they simply said good-bye as if they were coming back in a few hours, and drove away. Through the rear window they watched him standing with his housemates in the warmth of the California sun, smiling and waving until the car disappeared.

Homecoming

The following June, the family gathered at the airport on Elmendorf Air Force Base, anxiously awaiting the arrival of Jimmy's flight. Anxious questions and potentially disastrous scenarios filled Lionel's mind. "How," he wondered, "is Jimmy handling this, his first airplane trip alone, with no familiar people around to reassure him? Did my arrangements work out?" Lionel had tried to plan each stage to provide maximum coverage and minimum chance of mishap. He was pretty sure Lil got Jimmy onto the plane in Los Angeles; did Earl meet him in Seattle as planned and make sure he caught his flight to Anchorage? With his speech difficulties, had he been able to communicate adequately with the stewardesses? Did he have any understanding of why he was on a plane and where he was going?

Looking at the rest of his brood, another thought struck him: "The boys and Mary have grown so much, will he recognize them?"

Life had seemed strange that past year, without Jimmy around. Lil wrote faithfully each week, keeping the family abreast of Jimmy's life. She sent pictures; a favorite was of Jimmy in her yard on Christmas Day, wearing shorts! It was certainly a far cry from any Christmas he'd ever seen in Alaska. From all accounts, Jimmy had seemed content with his California school experience. As anticipated, he loved school, for which Lionel and Esther could only be thankful.

They received little in the way of correspondence from the school, except for bills. In addition to the tuition expense, extra services such as dental work and special therapies—all billed separately—added up to a considerable amount over the course of the winter, practically doubling the tuition cost. As the school year drew to a close, they reluctantly concluded that they could no longer afford the school's expenses. Lionel thought back to the Seattle doctor's dire warning that, if they chose not to institutionalize Jimmy, they would spend all their money looking for a cure. In all honesty Lionel had to admit that the doctor had a point; the cost of Jimmy's plane ticket home took about half of their remaining bank balance.

The plane touched down. Everyone leaned forward eagerly, all eyes straining to catch the first glimpse of Jimmy. Even his Grandma and Grandpa Haakenson were there from North Dakota, having extended their visit for one more day to welcome Jimmy home.

After a long wait, the door of the plane opened, and passengers emerged. Men, women, children climbed down the steps and crossed the tarmac toward the waiting crowd. But none of them was Jimmy. Lionel's worries started again. Where was he? Did something go wrong? Did he miss the connecting flight in Seattle? Uh-oh, the pilot and copilot were getting off...now here came the stewardess. She was holding the hand of a young boy...Jimmy! He'd arrived, safe and sound, looking much taller and grown up than he did when they last saw him in the fall. The look on his face, though, said that this was not one of his better days:

Jimmy's expression clearly revealed his misery and confusion. He had been with strangers all day. This morning in California Auntie Lil took him to the airport, turned him over to a lady who worked on the big plane, and then left him. The nice lady helped him find his seat, but she couldn't calm his fear when the plane started its engines. The roaring sound confused and scared him. He put his hands over his ears until the noise quieted down a little. The stewardess told him they were flying, and tried to tempt him to look out the window. He wasn't having any of that. Heights made him nervous.

The people on the plane were good to him: the stewardess gave him drinks and food, and brought comics and coloring books to keep him amused. When he acted tired, she brought a pillow and blanket so he could sleep. She even took him up to visit the pilot and copilot, who let him watch them fly the plane. Jimmy didn't care about how the plane worked; he just wanted them to take him home.

Auntie Lil said he was going home to Anchorage, but he'd begun wondering if she'd made a mistake. The plane landed once, and Jimmy thought he was home, but he wasn't. He was in a great big airport with lots of people and noise and confusion. Uncle Earl met him, and he was happy to see a familiar face. He hoped Uncle Earl would take him to Anchorage. But he just put Jimmy on another plane, and the engine noise started again. Now the plane had landed once more, and the nice lady took him by the hand. He hoped he didn't have to get on another plane. Was he never going to find Mamma and

Daddy?

The pilot and copilot said good-by, telling him what a good boy he was. He shook hands with them as he had been taught, but he couldn't make these people understand that he needed to find his parents. With tears blurring his vision, he followed dejectedly as the lady led him down the steps of the plane. His sorrowful eyes gazed at the crowd, seeing nothing but strangers. Loneliness and fear engulfed him.

As a man and woman walked toward him, calling his name, his eyes brightened. Daddy! Mamma! He let go of the stewardess' hand and ran to join his family. The sadness melted away as familiar, welcoming faces surrounded him. He's home, where he belongs.

Anchorage Schooling

For the next few months, my parents set aside thoughts of schooling and enjoyed the outdoor offerings of the short Alaskan summer. We eagerly anticipated going on Sunday afternoon picnics along Campbell Creek on the outskirts of Anchorage. On longer weekends, Lionel and a very-pregnant Esther loaded the car with kids, food, and gear and headed down to the Kenai Peninsula for some salmon fishing. Sometimes they stopped and camped along the Kenai River; other times they drove more than two hundred miles to fish the Anchor River in the tiny settlement of Anchor Point.

August brought the birth of another brother, Kenny, an addition that delighted Jimmy. A few days after she and the baby arrived home, Esther went to check on the infant, only to discover a vacant crib. She initiated a search of the premises, and soon found him in the back yard with big brother Jimmy. He was taking Kenny for a ride. After placing some blankets in the wheelbarrow, he had carefully laid the baby on top. Beaming at his own creativity, he trundled Kenny proudly around the yard.

With the approach of fall, came the recurrent problem of an appropriate education for Jimmy. He was now seven years old. The school in Los Angeles had excelled at teaching manners and daily living skills, but, to my parents' disappointment, Jimmy gained little ground in academic readiness. With no final report, they did not know if the school attempted to teach him reading and math and discontinued for some reason, or if the subjects had never been introduced.

Mrs. Thomas, a lady who attended church with our family and knew Jimmy well, informed my folks that she planned to start a private kindergarten that fall, and would welcome Jimmy. They thankfully enrolled him. The experience proved to be a godsend for Jimmy. Mrs. Thomas worked with him to learn colors, alphabet, and numbers. Expanding the letter recognition he started when sorting his pants from his brothers', he began learning to recognize the entire alphabet. He started sight-reading the names of students in his class, and writing letters, numbers, and his first name in uppercase letters.

By the end of the school year, the teacher felt that Jimmy

knew enough to succeed in public school. "Enroll him," she urged. That fall, he and Esther visited the nearby elementary school that Timmy attended. The first grade teacher, after meeting with them, enthusiastically welcomed Jimmy into her class. "I'll give him whatever extra help he might need in order to succeed," she assured my parents.

Then the principal got wind of the plan. He was a crusty old grump, who did not hesitate to voice his belief that no kid belonged in school until age nine. Someone with special needs certainly had no business showing his face at school. At the insistence of Esther and the teacher, he grudgingly agreed to let Jimmy enroll, but insisted the teacher watch him closely for any unusual or weird actions. "Write down anything he does that's not 'normal'," he commanded.

The teacher, bless her, did her best to treat Jimmy as one of the class, but with the principal constantly looking over her shoulder, the stress on student and teacher soon began to show. After just two weeks, my parents felt that the experience was too negative, and pulled Jimmy out of school.

Back to square one. How could Jimmy receive an education? Anytime someone gave him a chance, he demonstrated that, though slow, he was both willing and able to learn. All he needed was the opportunity and some additional instruction.

As was the case worldwide, Anchorage felt the blow when the polio epidemic hit in the '40s and '50s. The dread disease caused physical limitations for a number of young people, the numbers mounting sufficiently that the city created a school, known as the Crippled Children's School (CCS), to serve them. Through the Public Health Center, Esther learned of this school. Though its main goal was educating those whose bodies, rather than their minds, had limitations, the school agreed to take Jimmy as a student.

Esther, though glad the school accepted Jimmy, felt concern for the other students. Would Jimmy, not understanding their physical limitations, interact too roughly with those who wore braces or used wheelchairs? She soon found that her fears were groundless, as a typical day attests:

As the students work on a reading lesson, Jimmy follows along in his copy of the book, turning pages when the class does, studying the pictures as his classmates read. During handwriting practice, he laboriously prints his numbers and letters as he learned in kindergarten. He finishes by filling his tablet sheets with row upon row of scribbles, imitating as best he can the strokes made by his classmates. He loves coloring, too. Carefully watching the lines, he fills in the spaces with a rainbow of colors: a purple face, one arm green, one orange.

The teacher's voice breaks his concentration: "Boys and girls, gather around for story time." A frail little boy in a big wheelchair struggles to maneuver his unwieldy conveyance in the right direction. Jimmy springs into action. He carefully positions the wheelchair in the circle of children and sets the brake. He spots another classmate in leg braces, making her way slowly toward the teacher. Jimmy pulls out a chair and sets it where the girl can reach it easily. He continues his self-appointed job until satisfied that his classmates are comfortably seated around the teacher. Finally, he takes a seat himself.

This spirit of willing service came naturally to Jimmy and endeared him to teachers and students alike.

The Ice Cream Truck

*T*inkle, tinkle, tinkle. The distant sound wafted through the cool summer air. At first it was just a faint tickling in the ears of the four boys in the small yard. They were intent on their task—constructing a labyrinth of roads for an elaborate game of "Cars and Trucks." At least Timmy, Bobby and Johnny were constructing; nine-year-old Jimmy was trying out each new road with his own small car, complete with sound effects: "R-r-r-m-m-m-m...beep-beep!"

"Tinkle-tinkle-tinkle." The sound grew louder; the boys looked up, as did neighbor kids up and down the street. "Here comes the ice cream truck!" someone yelled. In every yard, youngsters rushed to their fences to watch, to wish. A few lucky ones actually stopped the ice cream man and bought a treat.

The boys in the Haakenson yard looked on from behind the white picket fence; they knew pretty well the answer, should they ask. Counting Mary and Kenny, who were playing in the house, there were now six children in the family. Not much money could be spared for extras like ice cream. It never hurt to ask, though. Johnny was dispatched to find Mamma–for a job like this, you always send the youngest available agent.

Hopeful eyes followed his progress to the house and, with fading optimism, his discouraged return. "She said no," he began, then looked around apprehensively. "Where's Jimmy?"

The three boys charged the house yelling, "Mamma! Jimmy's chasing the ice cream truck again!"

Esther dropped what she was doing. "Timmy, watch the little ones," she shouted, and set off in pursuit. At least she knew which direction to head. The fading "tinkle, tinkle, tinkle" acted like an emergency locator signal for her. Apparently for Jimmy it was an irresistible siren song. This was the third time he had escaped the yard and chased the truck, despite dire consequences each time.

As she sprinted down the road calling his name, Esther felt a mounting frustration. She knew something needed to change. The kids were growing so fast, it was getting more and more difficult to keep them within the confines of the small yard. Just the week before, the older boys ran off on an adventure; Mary followed them and got lost. Esther had been frantic by the time the police called to say that she was safe at the station with them.

Finally, Esther spotted a plodding figure in the distance. The ice cream truck had disappeared and from the body language, Esther saw that the thrill of the chase had worn off for Jimmy. She called him again; this time he heard. He turned around and waited.

As she marched him briskly back toward home, with her hand and his rear end smarting in unison from their recent meeting, she wondered why he did this. He had to know he was going to get into trouble. There had been other instances, too; twice recently he left the yard and Esther found him sitting in the general store, five blocks from home. Fortunately, everyone in the area knew him, but she knew it was still dangerous for him to wander off.

Esther and Lionel had discussed the problem of raising a large family on a small city lot. Both had grown up on farms with lots of outdoor room. They felt confined and knew their kids did, as well. Their house had twice acquired new rooms as the family grew, which only made the yard smaller. But what to do? Buying a larger property seemed beyond their financial abilities, since they both detested the thought of going into debt. "Cash on the barrel head" was their motto. And they recently had found out that a seventh child was on the way.

In this, as in all the difficulties they faced, my parents trusted in the Lord for their guidance. Both space and money were tight, but they knew that God would show them the way. As long as they waited for His time to be right, they knew the decisions they made would be right, as well.

In the fall, Jimmy eagerly returned to the Crippled Children's School. This year, both Timmy and Bobby were in the school run by the old grump, but not at the same time. Timmy attended classes on the early shift, and Bobby went for the afternoon. Jimmy's school offered his program in the afternoon, so transporting kids soon took up a major portion of our days.

The previously one-car family had to acquire a second vehicle to make it succeed. Lionel found a good deal on a Model A, which he drove to work, dropping Timmy off at school on his way. Esther gave the big Pontiac little time to rest or grow cold as she ferried children around the town.

"Okay, kids, it's almost time for 'Queen for a Day'," called

Mamma. We all knew what that meant: it was noon, and time to prepare for the daily rounds. Jimmy and two-year-old Kenny looked up from their morning's entertainment: spinning 45s on a small, kid-sized record player. Kenny was recuperating from a broken leg and needed something to keep him amused while immobilized. Jimmy loved music in any form, and played records for hours. What the records lacked in number and variety, the two youthful disc jockeys made up for in repetition. If they enjoyed a song the first time, then it must merit at least ten more playings. Regretfully, they shut off the machine. Since Kenny was unable to walk, Jim fetched both his and Kenny's coats.

After supervising and assisting the five of us into our outside gear, Mamma carried Kenny, with his cumbersome cast, to the car, and we piled in. The radio blared the day's election of the queen for the day as we sallied forth. At the grade school, our first stop, Bobby popped out and Timmy scooted in. From there, we drove to the homes of several of Jimmy's classmates whose parents lacked transportation. At each stop another child squeezed in with the rest of us. (In those days before mandatory seat belts and child safety seats, the car's inside measurements served as the only limit to its seating capacity.) We didn't mind a few extra warm bodies—a winter car ride is more comfy with passengers tightly compacted.

Finally, with the car stuffed to capacity and the trunk bristling with wheelchairs and crutches, we approached the Crippled Children's School. Jimmy and his classmates piled out, and Mamma headed home with her remaining children. A few hours later, she loaded us back into the car and headed out again to pick up Jimmy and friends. After delivering the non-family passengers to their respective homes, she picked up Bobby from school and headed home.

In her spare time, Esther managed to give birth to her seventh child, Ronny, in January of 1955.

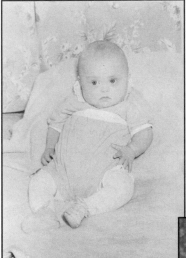

Above, baby Jim, age 8 months, was already showing signs of Down's syndrome, 1945.

Above right, Jim at 16 months, with his walker, 1946.

Above, Lionel and Esther Haakenson with baby Jim, 1945.

Tim, left, and Jim during the winter of 1949-1950.

Left to right, Jim, Robert and Tim display an early fascination with cars. Christmas, 1948.

Below, Mrs. Von Aspern, Jim (in front) and two other students outside the boarding school in Los Angeles, 1951.

Below, a sample of Jim's writing exercises, created during his brief time in school, 1954.

The Move

On an early May day in 1955, Lionel showed up as usual at the sheet metal shop where he worked. Nothing in the familiar surroundings offered a hint of the changes in our lives that would begin that day.

An apprentice who worked with him spoke up, "Hey Lionel, you like fishing in Anchor Point so much, how'd you like to buy a homestead there?"

"Buy a homestead? How do you do that?"

The man told Lionel about his neighbor, who had lived briefly in Anchor Point before deciding that the homestead life was not for him. (As the guy was a nightclub entertainer, it should have been a no-brainer.)

Interested, Lionel got the neighbor's address, told his apprentice to hold down the fort, and drove out to see him. This gentleman explained that it was not possible to "buy" a homestead; the only way to acquire one was to prove up by living on the land for a certain length of time. However, being anxious to dump such a remote piece of land, he said he would sell the improvements he had made on the property for $300. This just happened to be the amount of cash the guy needed to fly himself, his wife and daughter out of Alaska. Lionel checked his bank account and discovered that they had the $300, with about $50 to spare. Feeling it was a deal he couldn't pass up, he dashed home to sell the idea to his bride.

Esther was understandably surprised to see Lionel show up midmorning on a work day, and was even more amazed by his words, "How'd you like to move to Anchor Point?"

He related the events of the morning. Esther hesitated; this was a big step. She questioned him: was there electricity? He didn't think so. What about schools, doctors? He had little more information than she did, but was sure this was the answer to their prayers. Things would work out, if they just took this opportunity. Finally, with some reluctance, Esther consented, "All right, on one condition: that we'll have some sort of indoor toilet by winter. I'm not going to potty-train all these babies in an icy outhouse!"

This seemed like a minor point to Lionel, so he gladly agreed, then back to the seller he flew. By the end of the day, the papers were signed and he walked away, the proud new owner of largely unspecified "improvements" on forty acres of property he had never seen.

The conversations in the Haakenson home over the next week or so centered almost exclusively on the logistics of moving an entire household–which now included seven kids–to a location of unknown assets and liabilities.

Their few fishing trips to Anchor Point had been weekend outings spent in a tent or rental cabin on the Anchor River. Over the course of these visits my parents had garnered a few facts about the area, mainly that local legend claimed the explorer Captain Cook had lost an anchor in Cook Inlet, just off the mouth of the river, for which misfortune both river and town would forever remain memorials. Also, the town proudly held the dubious title of "Farthest West Point on the North American Highway System." Aside from those tidbits, Lionel and Esther knew very little, except that the rivers nearby were famous for their salmon, the area supported a healthy mosquito population, and two hundred and twenty miles of rough gravel road separated their present and future abodes.

As all good pioneers do, the Haakensons sent a party to scout out the area. This hardy band consisted of Lionel, Tim, and Robert. Tim, now nine, had grown into a sturdy, soft-spoken lad; at age seven, quick-witted Robert was always eager to be in the middle of whatever was going on. Jim remained home with Esther and the younger children. (In deference to their advancing years, the three oldest boys had dropped the childish endings to their names. Robert resumed his given name, due to the overabundance of Bobs and Bobbys among our friends and acquaintances.)

It was mid-May, so breakup was well underway. Breakup is a time of year that Alaskans anticipate with great ambivalence. We welcome it as the beginning of the end of winter, but dread it for the havoc it wreaks on our lives: rivers flood, houses moan and sag, and roads—well, roads have been known to disappear.

It happens every spring when warmer temperatures begin melting the frost that has permeated several feet below the surface of the ground. As it thaws, great mounds of mud push to the surface, leaving a hole the size of a small canyon under-neath. These mud mounds, known as frost boils, lurk on the surface of a roadway, camouflaged beneath a benign-looking film of dirt or gravel. When a car rolls unsuspectingly over one of these traps, the mud gives way, the tire falls into the hole, and the vehicle is suddenly very, very stuck. Often, several frost boils form in close proximity to each other. As a succession of vehicles drive over them, the area begins to more closely resemble a mud-wrestling pit than a road.

This was what lay in wait for Lionel and his sons as they embarked on that first journey to Anchor Point to check out the property. They left on Friday evening as soon as Lionel got off work, and began the eight-hour trek south. The first two-hour leg of the journey took them along a branch of Cook Inlet known as Turnagain Arm. On the right side of the road were the water and sand bars of the Arm. To the left were massive stone cliffs with cascading waterfalls, created as snow melted with the warming temperatures. Interspersed with the falls were deep chutes of snow where avalanches had slid during the winter.

Rounding the end of the Arm, the car started up into the mountains. The narrow, winding road took our adventurers over Turnagain Pass, across the Canyon Creek bridge with its tumbling waters a dizzying distance below, and into the little town of Cooper Landing, world-renowned for its salmon fishing streams. Just past this town was one of the most memorable parts of the trip to a youngster—a covered bridge over the Kenai River. It was dark and spooky, and just creaky enough to be terrifying in an exciting sort of way.

Finally emerging from the mountains, the road stretched on for fifty bone-rattling miles through a burned-over area containing few signs of human habitation, aside from the small hamlet of Sterling. Around midnight, the dusty car with its weary occupants reached Soldotna, the largest town they would see on this trek. From here, they had only sixty miles to go. Finally, at two o'clock in the morning—eight hours and two flat tires after they started—Lionel woke the boys and announced their arrival in Anchor Point.

So here the tired trio was, in the middle of the night, at the intersection of the highway and the North Fork Road (so named because it crossed the North Fork of the Anchor River about a half-mile from town.) According to the seller's instructions, they were almost there. The property lay just one and a half miles down the North Fork Road.

Did I say "just"? The frost boils on the North Fork Road, not content to have one or two others nearby, had formed entire neighborhoods, turning long stretches of road into oceans of sloppy goo.

Indeed, even calling the North Fork a "road" was somewhat of a misnomer; it was actually little more than a muddy path through the spruce trees, pushed out by someone's bulldozer.

Onto this questionable passage, Lionel and the boys eased the car in the wee hours of that Saturday morning. They soon fell into a pattern: drive a couple of feet, get stuck. Get out the jack, jack up the car, jam boards and branches under the tires, drive out. Go another few feet, get stuck.

Four hours—and a mile and a half—later, they arrived at the log house of Bert Paraday, a small wiry man, tough as a hunk of moose hide, whom we would come to call Uncle Bert. Bert welcomed the exhausted travelers, telling them that he had heard the noise on the road for the last hour or so, but thought it was just "some dern Cheechako gittin' stuck," so he had gone back to sleep. Lionel laughed. Having lived in Alaska for the better part of twenty years, he felt he was no longer a Cheechako (newcomer).

Bert offered Lionel a cup of coffee ("if I c'n find a spoon that ain't been licked"), then directed the three to the trail leading to their new property. The footpath offering the only access ran through Bert's yard, past his outhouse, across a swampy bog known as a "muskeg," then disappeared into the trees. He showed them where to leave their mud-spattered car while they tramped the last quarter mile of their journey on foot.

As they prepared to leave his cabin, Bert offered the use of his snowshoes. Lionel, fresh from Anchorage where the snow had all but disappeared, declined the offer. The boys were wearing hip boots, so he was sure they would be just fine. He soon realized that it pays to heed the instincts of the local residents. The path took them into the heart of a spruce forest. The sun that had warmed the road enough to bring out the frost had not managed to penetrate the woods. The accumulated snow from the previous winter had softened only enough to make walking arduous. With each step, their feet plunged deep into soggy, rotting snow. Lionel sank in above his knees, while the boys wallowed along with the snow coming almost to their waists. The hip boots proved more of a hindrance than help, as they filled with snow and added another dimension of misery to an adventure the high point of which, so far, had been a long and sleepless night.

With no reasonable alternative, the three persevered, and finally caught a first glimpse of their future home. In a small clearing, the view unmarred by such man-made trappings as electric poles and wires, stood the $300 "improvement": a 12-foot by 16-foot log shack. The crudely cut logs were chinked with moss, a commonly-used but relatively ineffective insulating agent. Apparently, at some previous time, the moss had filled out the spaces between the logs. It had since dried and shrunk, leaving large cracks between each log, through which mosquitoes buzzed merrily in and out of the house.

Inside the cabin, they found a wood-burning cook stove, but no wood. They were not staying long enough to need heat this trip, but the chainsaw would definitely have priority booking on the next visit. Using a kerosene lantern to light the corners (and aided by the early daylight that was already showing through the tiny windows and huge cracks between the logs) Lionel and the boys explored their new domain. In one corner of the single room was an open pit, which proved to be a hand-dug well; a glance down into the depths reassured them that they would have water. The level of the water could easily be determined by the mouse carcasses floating on its surface. Lionel made a note: first order of business, remove vermin and drain the well. Satisfied that water was available–if not immediately potable—they inventoried the remainder of the room: a homemade table, a crudely built bed, and the dried-out remains of a Christmas tree. Yes, a Christmas tree. The previous owner had fled the premises in the throes of a dark and frigid winter (possibly feeling it was the best Christmas present he could give his family), without taking time to remove the tree.

A ladder made of spruce saplings was nailed to one wall; the boys quickly climbed up and discovered an attic under the sloping eaves. Although obviously used previously for storage, there being only pieces of plywood laid across the rafters, the room offered Lionel reassurance that his offspring would have someplace to sleep other than the middle of the kitchen floor.

Out back, the guys found the toilet facilities; a log nailed between two trees formed the seat of the commode. Modesty was maintained by means of a piece of canvas, stretched around and nailed to surrounding trees. The doorless entrance to this rude edifice faced away from the cabin, allowing an occupant to gaze contemplatively out into the spruce trees, alone with his thoughts. Alone, that is, except for a million hungry mosquitoes. Having unobstructed access, these bloodthirsty marauders descended gleefully upon the hapless human balanced precariously inside. There they were guaranteed a feast, since it was impossible to swat mosquitoes and at the same time maintain one's perch on the pole. Lionel made another note: second order of business, build an outhouse.

Having satisfied (convinced?) themselves that the property had potential, the three succumbed to the effects of their sleepless night of unaccustomed activity, and curled up on the bed for a much-needed nap. Around noon, refreshed by a few hours' sleep, they reversed the whole process and returned to Anchorage to make their report to the rest of the family.

Perhaps they glossed over some of the details, or maybe the remaining $50 in the bank account spurred them to make something of their investment. Whatever the reason, two weeks later—on Memorial Day weekend—the entire family squeezed into our newly purchased station wagon, with what food, clothing and supplies could be tied to the roof rack, and made the move to the homestead.

Despite two additional weeks of spring weather, we youngsters still sank to our hips in snow as we trudged the trail to the cabin. It was just as well that the plan didn't call for us to leave the homestead often. Rather, Esther would get us settled in and start getting a feel for the new home while Lionel commuted each week to his job in Anchorage.

We did manage one trip to Anchorage that summer, in order for Mom to bring the old Pontiac down to Anchor Point. She wisely felt that it was unsafe to allow herself to be stranded on the homestead with seven children and no transportation. How well she knew her offspring.

On the Homestead

Almost before we finished unpacking, my parents began working on a 12-foot by 20-foot log addition that would more than double our current living space. Until it was finished, we staved off claustrophobia by spending as much time as possible outside.

When we gathered inside at mealtimes, we learned to tolerate the coziness. The table left by our predecessors was too small for us, so Dad attached a half-sheet of plywood to the top of it, making a 4-foot by 4-foot eating space. Temporary chairs were fashioned from chunks of firewood logs. An advantage of these chairs was the ease of customization. For the taller folks, the log was cut at normal chair height. Need a higher chair for a little tyke? Just cut a longer piece of log. With a short piece of 1-inch by 10-inch board nailed on top for a seat, the chair was complete.

At night, we six older kids slept on mattresses on the floor of the attic; five-month-old Ronny's "crib," a large cardboard box covered with mosquito netting, spent its days atop my parents' bed, and its nights tucked into a corner near the stove.

The weeks of that first summer soon acquired a rhythm that made maximum use of the available time and collective energy. About noon on Sundays, we all said good-bye to Daddy, and with Mamma's list in his pocket and a week's worth of dirty laundry over his shoulder, he tramped down the trail and headed for Anchorage. The laundry he delivered to Esther's sister Gladys. Given the primitive water-retrieval, heating and washing systems on the homestead, not to mention the overwhelming number of tasks to be done, Esther had struck a deal with Gladys to wash our clothes each week.

Lionel spent his weekday evenings employing his skill as a sheet metal worker to construct various items needed down on the homestead. A galvanized bathtub of his making reposed during the week against the side of the cabin. On Saturday evenings, it held center stage in front of the cook stove as we took turns making our weekly ablutions.

One of Lionel's first projects came about as a result of our lack of refrigeration. He fashioned a 2-foot-square box of sheet metal, and attached an insulated wooden door. Inserted through a hole he cut in the wall of the house, this became our cooler. The metal box stuck out from the outside wall of the house, shaded slightly by a lean-to that housed our wood supply. In other words, our "cooler" was possibly two degrees cooler than the current outside temperature. There are hidden advantages to living in a climate in which the summer temperatures rarely climb higher than the low 60s. Although this "Homestead-aire" was not suited for long-term storage of perishable goods, with a family of nine we rarely had leftovers, so that was not much of a problem.

Another weekend, Lionel showed up with a small rectangular metal box which he affixed to the side of the cooking range. It proved to be a small heater stove—an efficient way to heat the cabin quickly when firing up the big stove was unnecessary or too time-consuming.

In Anchorage, each Friday when Lionel finished work, he swung by Gladys' house and picked up the clothes—now clean and folded—packed the car with food, other supplies from the list, and whatever projects he had completed, and headed for Anchor Point. Arriving around midnight, he slept for a few hours. With help from Esther, Tim and Robert, he spent Saturday felling trees in the woodlot a short distance behind the house and building on the addition. On Sunday, the whole routine began again.

During the week, while Lionel was away, Esther literally kept the home fires burning. A typical day might go something like this:

"Johnny, I need some more firewood." Esther, as usual, is in high gear, moving through her tasks like a 97-pound whirlwind. Between trips to the window to check on the kids, she is trying to time her two most pressing chores–baking bread and washing diapers–to get both done in the most efficient way. She checks the vat of water heating on the stove. Turning to a large bucket on a nearby counter, she pokes the huge mound of bread dough billowing above its rim with an experimental finger. The dough is ready; quickly she kneads, rolls and plops six loaves into pans, and sets them to rise one more time.

Now for the diapers. Scooping water out of the vat with a big saucepan, she pours it into a galvanized washtub. She dumps the presoaked diapers into the tub, and begins to scrub them on the washboard. Just when she has a good rhythm going, Ronny begins fussing from his mosquito-netted cardboard crib. Great—he's probably readying another diaper for her at this very moment.

Drying her hands, she changes Ronny with the ease of one who can perform the task in her sleep, rinses the diaper in the pail reserved for that purpose, and tosses it into the wash water with its fellows. Rub-a-dub-dub: the nursery rhyme comes to mind as, up and down the washboard, she scrubs each diaper. Her back aches. She would give anything to have her wringer washer, but it is still in Anchorage, awaiting the day when electricity comes to the homestead.

Once the diapers are washed and rinsed, she hangs them on the clothesline that stretches between two trees in the front yard. "Well," she muses, "at least it's not raining." If it was, she would have to bring the damp diapers into the cabin in the evening and drape them over any available surface for the night. She takes the opportunity while she is outside to make sure all the children are accounted for. Although we have strict orders to stay within sight of the cabin, she knows that kids may forget such directives when absorbed in an interesting game. She is keenly aware of the fact that her eyes are not the only ones watching us. The woods surrounding our cabin are populated with moose, bear, and who-knows-what other wild beasties. Right now they are probably just curious about the small, noisy strangers who have invaded their habitat, but Esther is not taking any chances.

She finds Jim and us younger kids busy chinking between the logs that we are able to reach. Earlier, she had laid out long strips of fiberglass insulation; now, with the help of a small stick, we stuff the itchy fluff into the huge cracks between the logs. (At this time of year, it is not so much to keep out the cold; it's the mosquitoes entering uninvited that get Esther's goat.) Tim and Robert are out of sight, but she knows where they are: working on the logs down in "the woodlot," so named for its function as supply depot of logs for the house and wood for the stove.

Part of the process of proving up on the homestead entails clearing and putting under cultivation at least five acres of land. Each weekend, Lionel cuts down trees in the woodlot; then during the week, while he is in Anchorage, Tim and Robert peel the logs, readying them for use on the house addition. Once enough of the trees are removed, the area will be planted with potatoes and a few other hardy crops, in the hopeful expectation of receiving some sort of harvest.

Esther pins the last cloth to the line and races back into the house to check the bread. It's ready to bake. "Good," she notes, "Johnny remembered to bring in the wood." She pokes a few sticks into the stove's firebox and slides the pans into the oven.

A glance at the clock tells her that the kids will soon be wanting to know what's for lunch. She thinks wryly about the six loaves baking in the oven. They won't last long; this morning, at breakfast, the boys held a French-toast eating contest, each downing up to a dozen slices of bread. Now, for lunch, they will devour stacks of sandwiches as if they haven't eaten for days.

An impending meal means there'll soon be more dishes to wash. She sets Johnny to pumping water, and pours buckets into the depleted vat until it is full again.

Esther quickly assembles the lunch and dashes to the door of the cabin to summon the younger set. "Johnny! Get Jim, Mary and Kenny and tell them they'd better come in and start washing up. It's almost lunch time. Then go tell Tim and Robert to come up."

Racing back to the stove, she pulls the loaves out of the oven. The smell of freshly baked bread never fails to draw the kids in, wherever we happen to be. Jim, Kenny and I troop in, grubby and reeking of mosquito repellant. We take turns washing in the small basin of warm water Esther has set out. By the time we are all washed, the water resembles a mud puddle, but we are at least slightly cleaner than before.

Aside from the homemade bread, most of the ingredients of our lunch are things that have a fairly long shelf life and little need for refrigeration. In fact, our foodstuffs generally come in two forms: dried and canned. Our usual lunch consists of bread with peanut butter and jelly, some canned fruit and Kool-Aid. It all tastes good to us, and we dig in enthusiastically.

After lunch, we again disperse to our various appointed occupations. Tim and Robert return to peeling logs in the woodlot, Johnny to running errands and keeping an eye on Jim, Kenny and me. Our main job for the afternoon is to stay out from underfoot.

Often the task of keeping Kenny and me occupied falls to Jim. He is a very patient baby sitter, and willingly plays along with any game our imaginations invent. One of our favorites is

"Pet Moose," a true homestead kids' game. Kenny and I make up wildly improbable scenarios with ourselves as the heroes, while Jim plays the title role as our transportation. He crawls around on hands and knees for hours while we ride on his back.

Developmentally, Jim was probably near the same mental age as Kenny and me, though chronologically he was ten. As the younger siblings, we became unwitting participants in Jim's education, giving him continual practice in speech, interpersonal relationships, and daily living skills. Esther refused to let him off the hook when it came to completing his share of the chores, either. She had a good understanding of his abilities, and assigned jobs which were simple enough for him to carry out, but which were difficult enough to challenge his mind. As with the pajama lesson learned years before, once Jim knew what was expected, he carried through with few or no reminders.

As Esther finishes washing up the lunch dishes, she hears the soft voice of her second son behind her: "Mamma, I think I need a Band-Aid." Spinning around, she takes in the sight of Tim's hand, streaming blood. "I cut myself," he says unnecessarily.

Not from Tim will one see a childish display of tears and hysteria at the sight of his own blood. Though he had never received a full explanation of Jim's disabilities, Tim seems to realize that Jim is unable to fulfill the role normally expected of the firstborn. Quietly, and with a maturity beyond his years, Tim has stepped into the position, serving as Esther's right-hand man while Lionel is absent.

After the first thrill of panic subsides, Esther examines the cut while Tim explains what happened. He was picking his way through stumps, branches and generally lumpy terrain on his way to the next log to be peeled, when he tripped and fell. Oh, yeah; he was holding his two-handled skinning knife—known as a drawing knife—by the blade. Esther hates to see Tim and seven-year-old Robert handling such dangerous tools, but knows the work has to get done.

A quick assessment of the wound tells her that it is more than she can fix on her own. She is glad that the trusty old Pontiac is only a quarter-mile away, in Uncle Bert's yard. Wrapping Tim's hand as tightly as she can with a clean rag, she grabs Ronny out of his crib, and calls to the rest of us. Looking like a somewhat harried Pied Piper, she leads us down the trail. We pile into the car and make our way to the Mutches' cabin. Mr. Mutch is a pharmacist and his wife is a nurse. Between the two of them, they take care of most of the minor emergencies that arise among Anchor Point's residents.

The kindly, competent Mutches quickly treat the wound, assure Esther and Tim that he will survive, and send us on our way. No payment is requested or expected for these services. In a small community such as Anchor Point, everybody shares their particular abilities and talents, knowing that we are all dependent on each other.

That evening, with the Alaska summer sun beaming into the cabin as brightly as noontime, Esther is looking forward to getting to bed for a well-earned rest. The fire in the cook stove has been banked, and the scent of Buhach hangs in the air. (Buhach was an odoriferous powder that we burned as a smudge in the vain hope of discouraging mosquitoes from entering the premises.)

We kids are sponged off as well as possible, and have made our last-minute trips to the outhouse. Esther is about to send us attic-ward, when Robert asks, "Mamma, can we have a meeting?"

"Yeah! A meeting!" seconds Jim.

Looking at our hopeful faces, especially Jim's anticipatory smile, Esther agrees. Sitting with Ronny on her lap and the rest of us seated on the floor or draped across the few pieces of furniture, she lets us each pick a favorite hymn or Sunday School song. We belt out all our favorite hymns, making the quiet woods ring with old favorites like "In the Garden" and "This Little Light of Mine." Jim participates avidly, and when he begs us to sing "On a Hill Far Away," he isn't being rude—he just wants to sing "The Old Rugged Cross." Next the older boys recite passages of Scripture they have been memorizing. We younger kids have our own shorter verses that Mamma is helping us learn.

We end our "meeting" with a chain prayer. Mamma begins, then, one by one, we contribute our special requests or thank-yous to God for whatever is on our minds. This evening's prayer brings several expressions of thankfulness that Tim's hand is going to be okay.

When the prayer is concluded, we file sleepily up the ladder to our mattresses under the eaves. Esther settles down for a quiet time with baby Ronny, feeling she is lucky indeed that he is such a mellow little guy. Finally, when all is quiet upstairs and the baby is peacefully asleep in his box by the stove, Esther thankfully crawls into her bed. A day on the homestead: tiring, but never dull.

Thanks to the dedicated work of all parties involved, the addition was finished and ready to move into by late August. We felt as if we were living in a castle: all that room! A barrel stove made from a 55-gallon drum provided heat. My parents' bed and Ronny's crib finally could be moved out of the kitchen. A stairway led to a new, larger loft, which soon contained three sets of bunk beds, giving each of the rest of us a bed of our own.

The outhouse Lionel had built shortly after our move was palatial in comparison to the one that came with the place. It had four log walls, a door and two seats—one of standard height for the big folks and a shorter one for us little ones. However, he didn't forget Esther's request for indoor plumbing. Thus we became one of the first families in the area to have that most humble but appreciated of conveniences. It was only a 3-foot by 3-foot box in one corner of the new addition and had just one function, but it was the one that mattered. Washing, bathing, fixing hair—they could all take place in another location. A bucket set discreetly between the bathroom wall and barrel stove held gray water left over from household use. Any time a flush was needed, we dumped the water straight into the toilet, refilled the bucket and replaced it, ready for the next time.

In August, the electric company brought power to our area. Outages were frequent, but, in between, we appreciated the light and other benefits that electricity brought to our lives.

Education in Anchor Point

With September came the beginning of the school year. Johnny started first grade; Robert was in second, and Tim in fourth. The school in Anchor Point was a two-room, two-teacher operation. One teacher taught the first four grades; the other had grades five through eight. There was no kindergarten, no high school, and no accommodation for special needs. Tim, Robert and John were welcomed; Jim was turned away, sympathetically but with finality. The teachers had neither the training nor the inclination to admit him. The best my parents could hope for was to take him home and teach him as best they could. And that was that. At the age of ten, Jim had reached the end of his formal education.

This is not to say that all learning ceased. With so many siblings coming up behind him, someone was always learning something in which Jim wanted to participate. Whatever the current lesson was—whether school learning or life experience—Jim was sure to be in the middle of it. His educational experiences in California and Anchorage had given him a love of school that made it doubly hard for him to have to forego it.

In one of Lionel's first commutes home after our move to Anchor Point, he brought down Tim's and Robert's bicycles, which they spent their free time pedaling endlessly and recklessly along the trail that led to the woodlot back of the house. When they wanted even more thrills, they rode the footpath down to Uncle Bert's. It was studded with such pitfalls as tree roots, grassy hummocks, soft mossy spots, and mud holes. When Jim saw what fun the boys had on their bikes, he resolved to learn to ride, too.

Tim, Robert and John got to the point that they almost dreaded seeing Jim coming toward them, pushing one of the old but sturdy bicycles. They knew that one of them and Jim would be going a few more rounds with the bicycle, and, somehow, the bike always came out the winner. Throughout that first summer, and the next, and the next, the struggle went on. Grasping the seat, one of the boys would steady the bike, supporting most of Jim's weight as well. After a few feet, gravity would prevail, and they would land in a heap. For three long summers, this was the inevitable end to every episode. Then, when everyone but Jim had given up, finally—*finally*—it happened:

Jim mounts the bike with a look of determination on his face. He clutches the handlebars and puts one foot on a pedal.

John holds onto the back of the seat, making sure Jim is securely settled before shoving off. As always, John struggles to keep the bike upright; Jim's feet crank the pedals while his hands try to control handlebars that are suddenly doing a snake dance. The handlebars win again, and the bike crashes into a stump. Down they go in a tangle of bike and boy.

That was a bad fall; Jim comes up with a scrape on his arm and another on his forehead.

John quickly asks, "Are you okay?"

Without answering, Jim struggles to his feet; he yanks the bike free from the stump's roots, plants it firmly back onto the trail, and climbs aboard.

John figures, "Well, if he can keep going, so can I," and they set off again.

The two continue their halting progress down the trail. At first, the scenario looks a rerun of every ride of the past three years. Then comes a slight difference: Jim's hands begin to control the handlebars, instead of vice versa. The bike spends more time on the trail than in the berm. The distance between spills is getting longer. John is even able to let go of the bike seat momentarily. Jim's doing it! He's learning to ride!

Finally the moment comes when John lets go of the seat for the last time. Jim pumps the pedals, aims the only-slightly-wobbly handlebars down the trail, and rides.

One problem still remains: he has not learned to stop. The only way he has ever done that is by falling down or running into a stump. Well, that works; he willingly puts up with a few more bumps for the sheer thrill of riding. Eventually, he does learn to stop in the more generally accepted manner, and even to leap off the bike in mid-flight when necessary, as when lending a helping hand to the Lone Ranger.

Bike riding was a feat that even many of his family members believed he would never master. In this, as with so many other things, Jim believed in himself when almost no one else did, and proved everyone else wrong.

Another skill he saw his siblings accomplish that he was determined to learn, was telling time. John was, again, the teacher; this time his inspiration came to him during church.

With his eyes on the preacher, an expression of rapt attention on his face, John's mind is racing with the grand idea that has just struck him. He knows how to teach Jim to tell time! The cardboard clock–of course! Why hasn't he thought of it before? He wriggles on the seat, impatient to get home and put his theory into practice.

Once back home, John hunts up the cardboard clock on which he and the other boys had practiced their time-telling skills. Jim, always a willing pupil, sits earnestly studying the clock.

"See, you put the big hand on 12, and the little hand on 5. What time is it?"

"Twelve o'clock?"

"No, the little hand tells you the hour. It's 5 o'clock."

"Five o'clock?" Jim's face reflects his puzzlement.

This isn't going nearly as smoothly as it had in John's daydream. Jim recognizes the numbers, but is confused by the different functions of the big and little hands. John perseveres, though, patiently explaining the mysteries of time each day with the cardboard clock. Jim also picks up the clock on his own and studies it. At last the day comes when Jim can correctly name every hour and half-hour when shown on the clock. He begins telling time from the clocks around the house, as well, extremely proud of his new skill. John then expands to the quarter-hour, and finally, after months of work, to five-minute intervals. Jim never learned to count by fives, so his mastery of that level had to be strictly by memorization.

As with many of his skills, when I, then Kenny, and, finally, Ronny went through the clock-learning stage, Jim's nose was in there, learning everything he could right along with us. By the time he was finished, he could tell time to the minute. His extremely literal grasp on time meant that 9:23 was as different from 9:24 as it was from 4:56. All clocks in the house had to be set to the correct time, which was, of course, the time shown on his wrist watch. Listening to the radio for time checks became a daily ritual, with his watch being reset exactly with the radio several times per day.

An upside to this obsession was that we always knew at least one thing he'd need at Christmas time; he wore out several watchbands every year due to the pulling on and off, stretching, twisting and general mauling they received. With the daily setting, resetting, and overwinding, watches didn't last much longer.

Speaking of time, it often hung heavily on Jim's hands during the school year, especially once we younger kids started school. My parents were determined to help him learn to read. Though they had no training and no one to consult for direction, they were not totally without resources. They had one: an old *Dick and Jane* primer that the teacher of the younger grades thought she could spare. It was a start. Armed with the primer and a reel-to-reel tape recorder, my parents set out to create a reading program for Jim. They taught him to thread the tape, turn on the machine, and follow along in the book, using their recorded lessons. A lesson would go something like this:

"Open your book to page 1. See the 1? See the word at the top? That says 'Look.' Say 'look.' Now turn to page 2." Jim went over each lesson until he memorized the story, then went on to the next.

In my early primary years, I got swept away with the wonder of reading. I wanted Jim to experience that feeling, since I always felt he had gotten a raw deal by being barred from attending school. Sometime during my second or third grade, I took over the taping of Jim's reading lessons (Mom had managed to talk the teacher out of some elderly copies of the next few books in the series, once he finished the first one.)

After a stint with the tape recorded lessons, I finally felt confident enough to "go live." One Friday night, Jim and I made a date to sit down the next day and begin his "real school." I set out a small chalkboard, chalk, paper and pencil and the primer, and went to bed. Visions of Jim effortlessly reading swirled through my head as I lay trying to fall asleep. With this level of excitement, when I finally did fall asleep, I dreamed about our upcoming lesson. Unfortunately, my anticipation was so high that I pulled myself out of my dream, forced myself to wake up, and got up, unable to wait any longer.

With missionary zeal—but no idea what time it was—I trod over to Jim's bed. "Jim," I whispered, "*Jim!* It's time to start school." That last word was the magic one to Jim's ears. He awoke and allowed me to lead him through the dark, silent, chilly house to our "classroom." I am still amazed that Jim actually got out of bed, and believe it shows the lengths to which he was willing to go in order to participate in school.

That particular teaching session was short-lived, since our mother soon heard us and got out of bed to see what was going on. "You kids go back to bed," she whispered, "It's 3 o'clock in the morning!"

Sadly, I soon found that good intentions were not enough to make my dreams of teaching Jim to read come true. His speech challenges made the phonetic approach unusable, so he learned only words he could recognize by sight. Soon he began encountering words that were too similar in his eyes, such as "family" and "funny;" he was unable to distinguish between them, and we didn't know how to help him past this snag. This effectively ended his instruction in reading, though for several more years he continued to pull out his books and read them for the sheer enjoyment of the exercise.

The frustration and helplessness I felt in failing to teach Jim to read led directly to my decision to become a special-education teacher. Though I didn't know, at the age of nine, if such a field existed, I was determined to find out. Even at my tender age I was aware of the unfairness of the treatment Jim received from the school system. I could see that Jim was capable of learning; why couldn't others see it? I resolved that my life's work would be helping kids like Jim receive schooling that met their needs and prepared them for productive lives. Fortunately, I had excellent role models in my parents. They had no guidance for teaching academic skills to Jim, but they needed no guidance to teach life skills. And, in the final analysis, those skills served Jim best.

Though Jim never became what anyone would term "a reader," he picked up–chiefly through his own initiative and persistence—a number of sight words that were meaningful to him. Among these were the names of the months and days of the week, which he learned thanks to his obsession with the calendar. With a family of nine people, birthdays came around frequently. This may have been the source of his original interest, but he soon took calendar watching to a whole new level.

At the beginning of each year, Jim thumbed through the calendar, studying each month and locating the birthdays of all family members, all the major holidays, and any other dates that were important for him. He then regaled us with much more information than we wanted about each date ("My birthday is May 9—it's on Saturday.") He became our infallible calendar expert. Once he had gone through and located all the relevant data, it remained locked in his mind for the rest of the year. If we needed to know anything about a particular date, we found it just as quick–and accurate–to ask Jim as to look it up on the calendar: "Hey, Jim–when's Mom's birthday?"

"July first–Friday; she's gonna be 46," he would fire back without missing a beat. It was as quick and uncomplicated as that. I think he often wondered what was wrong with us that we could never remember something so ridiculously simple.

Toothpicks

We sit in the kitchen with all the lights turned out, crammed together on homemade benches circled around the plywood table. We wish we could make the room a little darker, but it's May. No place around here is ever really dark this time of year. In the soft light, the seven of us can be seen, the height of our heads proclaiming our ages. Jim's and Tim's heads are roughly even. Robert's is next, then John's, then mine. Kenny's little face peeps over the table's edge. Ronny bounces in his high chair, impatient to get on with the party. Our eyes reflect the glow of the candles sprouting from the cake that sits in sugary splendor on the special "birthday plate." Our vigorous rendition of "Happy Birthday" resounds through the cabin while Jim, the birthday boy, sits smiling proudly, and a little self-consciously, obviously anticipating the moment when he will claim his slice of cake.

Birthdays on the homestead gave us an excuse for a party. Not having access to fast food places or mobs of friends with whom to celebrate, we made the best of our circumstances and had a good time, anyway. After all, seven kids is a fair-sized party. As Jim awaited the cutting of the cake, he knew, as did we all, that the real meaning of a birthday was not the treats, the number of guests, or even the presents. No, it was really all about toothpicks.

Yes, toothpicks. Our mother never wanted the birthday kid to have exclusive attention. And, knowing the joy little ones derive from the smallest surprise, she started a creative but inexpensive tradition to add an extra touch of fun to our celebrations.

The everyday cake in our family differed from the birthday variety. Because of the speed with which it disappeared, the run-of-the-mill cake was dumped into a rectangular pan, baked, and slathered with a simple vanilla or chocolate frosting, made primarily from margarine and powdered sugar. Time was a precious commodity, and wasting it on a cake that would be gone as soon as supper was finished made no sense to my mother.

A birthday, though, called for a little more effort. After baking the birthday cake in two round layers, Mom made her special frosting of egg whites, sugar and corn syrup. She called it "Seven Minute Icing," and it had to be beaten for what seemed to me at least seven hours in the top of a double boiler. She then added a few drops of food coloring, tinting it to the stated specifications of the one whose birthday was being celebrated. The leftover frosting she tinted another color to use for piping flowers and the words "Happy Birthday" on top as a finishing touch.

But before the frosting came the fun part: she colored three toothpicks—one blue, one yellow, and one red. These she inserted into the stacked cake layers, which she then frosted, covering all traces of the holes made by the toothpicks. We knew that a blue toothpick found in our piece of cake netted us a shiny nickel; the yellow was worth a dime, and the red brought in a quarter.

The thrill of finding a toothpick in one's piece of cake almost eclipsed the honor of being the one whose birth precipitated the event. Whereas most small children, when given a slice of cake, immediately lick off the frosting and ignore the cake entirely, we went right to the heart, splitting the piece horizontally, searching for that sliver of wood that proclaimed someone a winner. The cries, "I got one!" "I got the red one" were greeted by what we hoped were sportsmanlike smiles from those who didn't win, this time. On the bright side, with nine people in the family, sometimes we waited only a week or two, but rarely more than a month, before the next birthday rolled around.

Jim's search for the toothpick usually was a more protracted affair than that of the rest of us. If, upon splitting his cake in two no toothpick popped up, he carefully ate a few crumbs at a time, his entire attention riveted on his quest. An archaeologist seeking fragile artifacts could be no more careful than Jim as he dissected that cake, holding onto hope until the last bite disappeared.

His disappointment exceeded ours as well, which must have tempted Mom from time to time to slip an extra toothpick into his piece; after all, an extra nickel or dime would be a small price to pay to give him a happy moment. She did not succumb to such temptation, though, and I believe there were a couple of reasons why. For one, little kids are the world's guardians of fairness. It wouldn't have taken many birthdays for us to figure out that Jim was receiving special treatment. Our outrage at such a show of favoritism might well have brought undeserved retribution on his innocent head. Also, Mom believed, in this instance as in others, that she needed to allow Jim to experience disappointment. Otherwise, having things too easy would lead him to expect life to go his way without working at it. She knew, in the long run, fostering such an attitude would be a huge disservice to him, just as it would have been to any of the rest of us.

Bossy

Hang on, Robert! Don't let her get away!" Clutching a knot at the end of the rope, Robert flew through the air like a long, oddly shaped satellite around the small, feisty Holstein attached to the other end. But he hung on. A small cluster of men and boys swarmed around, trying to shoo the cow up the ramp into the trailer that would transport her to our place, her new home. She was just as determined to escape the whole scene. Eventually the human element prevailed, and the cow stood unhappily in the trailer, huffing noisily through her nose.

So, three years following our move to Anchor Point, our family became cattle wranglers. The former owners had named the little cow "Mary," which I found highly flattering. My mother took exception to having her daughter answering to the same name as the family bovine, though, so we wracked our singularly uncreative brains and came up with a new name: Bossy.

Until the advent of Bossy, our milk was of the powdered variety that had to be mixed with water. Powdered milk of that era was prone to clumping in large, hard lumps, which my little brother Ronny loved. He would snitch several of these lumps from Mom for a snack, which he shared with the family cat, Tommy. I had quite an opposite reaction to those lumps. Even when they were mixed with water, I felt the resultant concoction bore a revolting dissimilarity to the real thing, so I welcomed the arrival of the cow.

Bossy became the sole source of milk for our family and several of our neighbors. In the course of time, she was replaced by Popeye and, finally, by Daisy. These three, though I feel sure they never set hoof inside a school building, taught Jim lessons that served him well throughout his life.

Support of a milk cow in Alaska requires a major commitment of money. Much of the year, all feed has to be bought and provided by the cow's owners. A barn must be built to store said feed, as well as provide a place to milk the cow and shelter her during the bitterly cold days of winter. And, as is the case with milk cow owners everywhere, there is a time commitment; we found it necessary to adhere to a fairly rigid schedule. My parents felt both the expense and time were worthwhile investments. They believed that responsibility was good for kids, and that upkeep of a cow would help make us better people.

We each played a part in cow care, based on our ages and abilities. For several years, Tim, Robert and John took turns with the milking, feeding and watering chores. The rest of us kept the cow groomed and supervised her grazing during the summer.

My parents knew that the short Alaska summer, with its abundant grass for grazing, would soon give way to a long, cold winter, when deep snows covered all trace of self-service forage. To supplement the expensive hay and grain we needed to stock for the winter, Dad planted several acres of oats in the newly cleared field we still referred to as "the woodlot." This also fulfilled the homesteading requirement to have at least five acres of land under cultivation. Each fall we harvested the crop and packed it into our homemade silo for winter cow feed.

Since the woodlot lay a mere hundred yards or so behind the barnyard, it was a simple thing for Bossy to nip down the trail through the woods and gorge herself on the tender shoots of oats. Like many humans, once she went on a binge she didn't know when to stop. But unlike humans, her excesses put her in danger of bloating, which could have killed her.

As this would seriously impact the amount of milk she produced, Jim, Kenny, Ronny and I were charged each summer with the responsibility of making sure Bossy stayed out of the oats. My two younger brothers and I sometimes got caught up in games and forgot about the cow, but Jim was faithful in his vigilance. More often than I care to admit, Jim reminded us of our responsibilities when he came running up the woodlot trail, bellowing that Bossy was in the oats.

When school started, many of the responsibilities we shared during the summer fell to Jim, since he was the one left at home. This was fine with him. He reveled in his jobs, and guarded them jealously. Somehow, within a very few years, he managed to edge his brothers out of the milking chores (not that they put up too much of a struggle). The structure necessary to keep a cow on a good schedule was just what Jim craved. Instead of heading out to milk "early" in the morning and "in the evening" he assigned times: 6:00 in the morning and 6:00 in the evening.

To Jim, these times were not negotiable. For the morning milking, he got himself up and out to the barn. Many a morning, before anyone else was stirring, Jim arose, milked the cow, then strained and put the milk away. He was equally dedicated to the evening milking, though there were more pitfalls in his path. These pitfalls usually took the form of one or more of his family members, especially if we all were away from home when the evening milking time drew near. Along about 4:30 Jim began to fidget. After a half-hour or so of silent but continual clock-watching, he hunted up Dad from whatever he was doing, and gave him a gentle reminder: "Pa, it's 5:16." If Dad didn't move quite as fast as Jim thought he should, he became a little more direct: "I gotta go home and milk the cow." If even this failed to get folks moving, he began to get irritated. He paced the floor (purposely remaining within eye- and earshot of Dad), and mumbled to himself: "It's time to go home...I gotta milk the cow...it's 5:22...Pa's not coming...it's late...it's 5:24..." Finally Dad threw up his hands in defeat, home we went, and the cow got milked at the appointed hour.

Jim's connection with animals sometimes transcended our understanding. Several times his insistence that we go home was not because of milking time. Instead, he stated firmly, "Bossy's loose." Receiving a scoffing reply or an unbelieving glance, he kept it up: "We gotta go home. The cow's gone." Sure enough, when we got home, Bossy was nowhere around. We quickly fanned out to search and, luckily, always managed to find her enjoying a few moments of illicit freedom in the garden or munching fern roots somewhere in the woods.

Jim seemed to inspire a trust in our livestock that was truly special. Our last cow, Daisy, had a bull calf that we named Buster. (In fact, I believe we named all of our bull calves Buster.) This particular calf played a butting game with our youngest brother, Ronny, who was about nineteen at the time. Ronny would push the calf's forehead, the calf would push back, dance away, then come back and butt against Ron's hands again. They both enjoyed the game at first. Ronny, lean and muscular from four years of high school wrestling, had a kind of macho thing going, pitting his strength against the growing Buster.

However, as Buster entered adolescence, he began to resent this aggravating human who still wanted to push on his head. He soon transferred his annoyance to just about anybody who ventured near, attempting to charge anyone who tried to enter the barnyard. Anyone, that is, except Jim. When Buster snorted and waved his head threateningly, Jim calmly approached him, cuffed him affectionately on the neck, and told him, "Now, Calfie, cut that out." Belligerent

Buster, suddenly transformed to meek Calfie, followed Jim like a puppy dog, a look of goofy adoration on his face.

Bossy, and her sisters that succeeded her, did more for Jim than just give him a schedule and a reason to tell time. We put the milk up in glass gallon-size containers. These were obtained by the simple expedient of buying all possible items—from mayonnaise and pickles to peanut butter–in gallon jars and reusing them as milk jugs. Our customers' dairy needs varied by the size of their families, so we planned accordingly. For instance, if Family A needed one gallon twice a week, and Family B got two gallons three times per week, we marked and set aside the appropriate amount for each customer. We operated a cash business–$1 per gallon. Jim became proficient in dealing with customers. Sometimes when we were all in school, if Mom had to run an errand, she would take Jim to the cooler and point out the jars:

"If Blanche comes, give her this one. If Ruth comes, she gets these two."

Jim thrived on this sort of responsibility. He greeted customers, handed over the correct jars of milk, took the money, and put it away carefully in the cupboard, ready to turn over to Mom when she returned.

The cow-care experience also helped Jim cultivate an ability to solve problems, as a story told by our friend Wallace illustrates. As Wallace and his wife, Mary, sat visiting with my parents, through the window they could see Bossy's half-grown calf, Beauty. She was tethered to a running line strung between two trees in the yard. Soon the adults realized that poor Beauty couldn't move. The rope attaching her to the running line was snarled around the tree trunk, roots, branches and her legs. She looked as if she'd tried to play a complicated game of "Cat's Cradle" with the tree.

Lionel called, "Jim, go untangle the calf." As Jim unhesitatingly set off on his mission, Wallace wondered to himself, "Why is Lionel sending his retarded son on a job like this? He's got all those other big boys who could handle it much easier." As a Texan, Wallace had worked with cattle, and knew the strength and skill it took to throw a calf the size of Beauty, then hold it down while untangling the rope. He seriously doubted that Jim could manage it all.

His ready sympathy stirred, he sat poised and ready to run

to Jim's assistance if the job proved too difficult. To his surprise, Jim made no attempt to throw the calf. Walking to the running line, he unclipped the end of the rope. Carefully he threaded it back around calf and tree, legs and roots, retracing its path until it again hung free. He re-clipped the rope's free end to the running line, patted Beauty on the rump, and the job was complete.

"Wow," thought Wallace, "And we consider *him* retarded."

Despite Jim's capacity for solving such everyday problems, mastery of basic academic subjects continued to elude him. We tried, unsuccessfully, for years to help Jim grasp the concept of addition. He could count objects, though he began to get confused if there were more than about twelve. On a good day, he could rote count to thirty. With no training, we were unable to get across to him the concept of adding more to a number to make another number.

A few years after Bossy joined the family, our parents acquired Jim's next set of unorthodox teaching assistants, namely seven Rhode Island Red hens. The septet divided naturally into three distinct groups. The five egg producers we named Short Wings, Curly, Speckles, Moose and Gladys (so named because she sounded like our aunt Gladys). A sick hen who slept most of her abbreviated life away inherited the name Alice from Mom's older sister. Aunt Alice was notorious for falling asleep in the middle of a conversation or just about any activity that put her into a sitting position. Finally, there was Bossy. Not the cow—the chicken. (Did I mention our lack of originality in the naming department?) Bossy-the-chicken apparently thought she was a rooster. She strutted around, refused to lay eggs, and ruled with pecks and threatening clucks, which thoroughly cowed her coop mates.

By the time the chickens arrived on the scene, much of Jim's attention was taken up with the cow, so he didn't, at first, have a great deal to do with their day-to-day care. That task fell to me, with assistance from my younger brothers, because I discovered an unexpected affinity for the silly creatures (the chickens—not the brothers).

Until we acquired our chickens, I mistakenly believed that eggs were always laid in the dead of night. In books I had read, people always went out to the hen house early in the morning to collect the eggs. Apparently, those book people didn't have the fascination with the egg-laying process that we kids did. We knew to the second when each egg was laid since we usually were lying in wait to grab it as soon as it popped out of the chicken.

We brought the fresh eggs into the house and put them on the counter to be washed before boxing them up and putting them away. It was fun to bring them in throughout the day and keep track of how many we got.

Jim got as big a kick as any of us out of bringing in the eggs. I credit those chickens and our simple egg counting routine for Jim's eventual understanding of basic addition.

If we had collected two eggs earlier in the day, and he came in with three more, he would line them up carefully on the counter, and count them all. Then he'd announce to the world at large, "We had two eggs; we got three more. Five eggs today!" Counting and adding those eggs gave him a real, concrete way to use and understand a previously unfathomable skill.

His grasp of mathematics never advanced beyond the simplest of addition and counting; for instance, money's value remained a mystery. He recognized the various coin and bill denominations, but saw no difference in value between one dollar and one hundred, or a penny and a quarter.

His lack of money sense would have worried us more, except that all his money dealings took place either at home or within our small community. We knew we could trust the local folks to treat Jim with honesty and respect, regardless of his understanding.

We used to have movies in the community hall for an admission of fifty cents. Years later, inflation pushed the price up to a dollar. The first time that Jim wanted to attend the movie after the increase, Mom tried to prepare him for the change in admission price. To Jim, such a change seemed frivolous and, therefore, he refused to believe it. Each time she told him it would be a dollar, he stubbornly shook his head and insisted, "Fifty cents."

She gave him a dollar anyway, and he blithely went off to the show. When he got home, Mom asked him, "How much did it cost to get into the movie?"

"Fifty cents," he said smugly.

"Did they give you two quarters back?" she queried.

"They forgot!" he replied laughing, obviously feeling the joke was on them.

Meeting the Bus

A solitary figure stood at the bus stop in the blackness of a winter morning, eyes and ears straining. He looked back toward the trail. "Where are the kids?" he muttered. "They're gonna be late." His eyes swung around to peer up the road. He was watching for lights at the corner just up the road a ways. Generally, few cars frequented the road at this time of the morning, so any lights he spied would probably be the bus.

What's that? He thinks it is...he's pretty sure...yes! Lights! "BUS!" Jim bawled at the top of his lungs.

His siblings, hearing the dreaded yell, stepped up the pace from their various points along the quarter-mile-long trail. I, as usual, was bringing up the rear. This was not entirely my fault: my mother, for some obscure reason, was determined to send her only daughter to school each day looking like a girl. This added precious minutes to my morning routine while she primped and fussed over me. I then spent the next six or seven hours undoing her handiwork.

I galloped down the dark, slippery driveway, my carefully curled and beribboned hair stuffed up into the hood of my parka. The front skirt of my lovingly homemade dress with its starched frills was crammed into my snow pants. The back half hung out, flapping as I ran. For the hundredth time I wished I could be like my friend Chris. Chris had beautiful long black braids and wore overalls with flannel shirts. She probably got dressed and to the bus every day on time.

Jim's bellowing call continued with a regularity that created a cadence for my running feet: " BUS!" (two, three, four, five, six, seven, eight); "BUS!" (two, three, four...). I was slightly comforted by the sound of his yells, because once the bus stopped at the driveway, he'd quit calling.

Uh-oh—silence. I skidded around the final corner just in time to see the last of my school-bound brothers disappearing up the bus steps. Well, technically, I was not late, since I was within sight of the bus before everyone else was seated. Panting, I scooted onto the bus and flung myself into the seat beside Chris of the exotic braids and envied overalls.

As the bus pulled away from our stop, I looked back, and in the glow of the bus's taillights I saw the shadowy figure of

Jim standing alone, watching us leave. Jim, our bus early-warning system. Jim, who faithfully saw us off each morning and was often the only one to get to the bus stop on time. Jim, who would have walked to the road naked and barefoot through the snow, for a chance to ride the bus. But he couldn't ride, because "people like him" were not welcome in school.

One morning we had all managed to make it out the driveway on time. As we stood waiting for the approaching bus to stop, Jim suddenly pulled off his boot and peered intently into it. Robert, with an adolescent's horror of acknowledging even well-behaved family members—let alone those doing something that looked a little odd—growled, "Jim, put your boot on. They're gonna see you." Jim put his boot on, we boarded the bus, and thought no more about the incident.

Meanwhile, Jim made his way back home and burst into the cabin, his normally small eyes seeming to fill his entire face, exclaiming, "Mamma, I got a mouse in my boot!"

Ever practical, Mom replied, "Well, take it off."

He did so, and out tumbled a still-alive but no doubt traumatized mouse. Its freedom was short-lived, as the family cat quickly pounced, bringing its short, eventful life to a violent end.

Sunday Sprint

I mentioned earlier that, by the time the doctor informed them of Jim's condition, my parents had discovered that Jim had the ability to learn. Even after they knew of his disability, they kept their expectations as closely aligned as possible with the other members of their rapidly expanding family. I guess, when a new baby comes along every year or so, parents just don't have time to continue doing all the basic self-help chores for anyone who's old enough to do them for himself.

Mom has often commented that she believes the greatest help in raising a child with disabilities is to provide that child with a host of siblings. Aside from being continuous models of typical (which is not to say perfect) behavior, siblings provide challenges and entertainment in ways a parent never could.

Dressing skills are a prime example. In my work as a teacher of children with disabilities, I've encountered children in just about every stage of acquisition of this simple but important skill. In a typically developing child, along about the age of two a parent begins to hear something like, "I do it myself!" From this point, it's not long before that child is dressing independently.

Children who experience disabilities often need help for a much longer time and even when they are able, it seems quicker and more efficient for an adult to do it. Many of these children do not make a big fuss to do it themselves, so the parent continues to dress them long after they have the ability to do it on their own. Although in the short term this saves time and possibly even avoids some brawls, in the long run everybody loses. The adult remains locked into the task of dressing the child, or finding someone else to do it; the child is denied greater competence, as well as the feeling of pride that comes with taking one more step toward independence.

I can't remember a time when Jim had to be helped getting dressed. As part of a rambunctious crew of youngsters, he was never singled out as the one who "couldn't" when it came to dressing. We had a Sunday afternoon ritual that, I'm sure, inspired him to an even greater degree of independence in this area. As soon as we got home from church, we were required to change out of our good clothes. Being as fond of rivalry as any siblings, we soon turned this into a race to see who could get changed the quickest.

The rules were simple: articles of clothing could be loosened while still in the car, but nothing could actually be removed until one was out of the car and on the way into the house. And before anyone could yell, "I'm done!" the Sunday-go-to-meetin' clothes had to be neatly hung up or put away in a drawer. It's a good thing our yard was secluded enough that the neighbors weren't witness to the sight—the seven of us in various stages of undress, piling out of the station wagon, jostling our way into the house and taking the stairs two or three at a time on the way to our rooms. Some of my brothers were not above a little sabotage to slow their rivals. This generally took the form of simple sibling mistreatment such as pushing and tripping. A few dastardly deeds took more preplanning, like sneaking into another's room before church to tie the sleeves or pant legs of the play clothes together, or buttoning up all the buttons of the competition's shirt.

Jim never got involved in such shady doings; he wouldn't have thought to treat us like that, and we, though we didn't completely understand why he was the way he was, wouldn't take advantage of him in quite that way. He was right in the thick of competition with us, though, and sometimes won the race, probably because he was not involved in the extraneous scuffles. Each time he participated in the "Sunday Sprint," he was learning to be a faster, more efficient dresser, and the expectation was reinforced that every member of the family was responsible for his or her own dressing, as well as care of clothing.

Years later, during the time I attended college in Greeley, Colorado, Jim visited me and attended a camp run by Easter Seals for those with special needs. He had never had an opportunity to do anything like this before, and I wondered how he would adjust. I needn't have worried. He had a great time doing all the things that campers do, from hikes and nature lessons to songs around the campfire. The final evening was Awards Night; Jim won the award for "Best Dressed Camper." His counselor (who obviously had never been informed about the neatness gene) told me in amazement how he watched Jim carefully unpack and hang or fold his clothes, and put them tidily away. All week, his clothes were never carelessly tossed, but always returned to their appointed places. At the end of the week, he placed all the items back into his suitcase, independently and neatly. Indeed, the pajama lessons and the Sunday Sprint had enduring and far-reaching value.

Fishing Site

The years rolled along, bringing changes to the homestead as it matured along with our family. We acquired an extra sixty acres of land, bringing the total to an even hundred. The footpath with its terminus in Uncle Bert's yard was replaced by a trail of our own some few hundred yards from the old one. This began as a muddy path, then upgraded to a drivable trail and, finally, thanks to years of grooming and tons of gravel poured into the frost caverns, attained the title of Driveway. The surface was still graveled, and bumpy enough to send a car's occupants airborne if driven at speeds in excess of 3 mph. (I know of one family whose favorite part of a visit to our place was zooming in the driveway.)

We kids sprouted up, too, eventually losing the distinction of "oldest is biggest." Robert, John and Ken all ended their growth at an inch or more over six feet. Tim and Ron stopped slightly short of that magic number. I, once I realized the futility of keeping up with my main rival, John, leveled off at a relatively stubby 5' 7". Jim, shorter than his brothers thanks to the effects of Down's syndrome, stood almost exactly the same height as I. To my chagrin, the two of us often were closer than I would have liked to the same weight, as well. We also wore the same shoe and coat sizes. This phenomenon came in handy when shopping for presents for Jim. I could try on prospective articles of clothing and have a pretty good idea if they'd fit him.

The log cabin, after three additions, was abandoned for a new house, which we spent a year building, just across the yard. We moved in Thanksgiving Day of 1960. The new house had hot and cold running water and a real bathroom, with a toilet that flushed without the aid of a bucket. The bathroom also contained a sink and bathtub, allowing us to wash somewhere other than in the middle of the kitchen. (I don't recall a single tear being shed at the retirement of the old galvanized tub.) However, even with its many conveniences, we were discouraged from lingering unnecessarily in the new bathroom, as we outnumbered it nine to one.

This home was, without a doubt, a major upgrade from the cabin. A vast expanse of combined living and dining areas lay just inside the front door. Beyond the dining room, the kitchen boasted a large double sink and lots of cabinets. A new propane range stood in the kitchen, offering a much more even cooking temperature for everything from boiling water to roasting a turkey. An oil furnace in the basement heated the house with a mere flick of the thermostat. Being frugal by nature, my dad installed florescent lights in all the rooms except the basement. Many people consider this type of lighting cold and unwelcoming, but we appreciated the brilliant beams, especially during the long, dark winters.

Hardwood flooring throughout the main part of the house offered a virtually indestructible surface, capable of standing up to the everyday abuse of tracked-in mud and snow on countless feet. It also had to withstand less common but more potentially destructive occurrences, such as water wars. In these fights, squirt guns were scorned as "sissy stuff." My brothers much preferred to wage war by the bucket- and dishpanful.

My parents' bedroom was on the main floor, down a short hall behind the kitchen, next to the only bathroom. The rest of us slept either in the basement or the upstairs. We moved from room to room for awhile, until each found the spot most suited to his or her comfort zone. Robert staked out a small upstairs alcove as his private space. Ken and Ron shared a room next to Robert while Jim, Tim and John took the bedroom in the basement. I, as the only girl, got a room of my own. (This did not indicate undue favoritism, by the way. My parents had an aversion to the idea of spoiling any of their children, and we all received fairly equal treatment, whether we were male or female, gifted or disabled. A separate room was strictly a matter of practicality, as I'd soon be too old to continue bunking with the guys.)

A major piece of kitchen furniture began its life as a section of the house's plywood siding. When Dad framed the hole for the front doorway, he saw potential in the large, rectangular cutout. Some sturdy legs, a wood trim to cover the rough edges, and a few coats of varnish transformed it into a plain but serviceable kitchen table, just the right size for seating a family of nine.

One convenience our new home lacked was a refrigerator. To compensate, we had two alternative appliances. First, Dad constructed another cooler similar to, and possessing the same limitations as, the "Homestead-aire" he had built for the cabin.

In the winter, things froze in it, and in summer, they got too warm. For the gallons of fresh milk the cow produced, we required an appliance capable of maintaining a more consistent temperature. Dad filled this need by adapting a small chest freezer whose automatic switch had mysteriously gone haywire, possibly due to some little fingers poking sticks or other foreign objects in where they didn't belong. He rigged the freezer up to a manual switch on the wall, so we could cool the unit by flipping on the switch, setting a timer, then flipping it back off when the timer rang. This took much greater vigilance than a regular refrigerator would have, but it sufficed for our purposes and remained our primary means of keeping things cold for many years.

Another thing we didn't have was a telephone. They were becoming more common in the area (I believe there were four in Anchor Point at that time), but it would still be more than a decade before we acquired one. We communicated with distant friends and loved ones by letter. As for those nearby, well, we just waited until we saw them.

The move into that new house ushered in what were, for us, major lifestyle changes. The oil furnace and propane cook stove made splitting wood unnecessary. As chopping wood had taken up a good bit of the older boys' time and energy, it wasn't long, even with their cow care chores, till they found time beginning to hang heavy on their hands.

Anchor Point in the '50s and early '60s was not a hotbed of sheet-metal activity (or any other activity, for that matter). When the job he had in Anchorage ended, Dad found it necessary, during our early homesteading years, to accept other jobs with the union, which took him far away from home. The statewide communication system, known as the White Alice system, was under construction; he flew to many of these sites throughout the state, from Sitka in southeastern Alaska to White Mountain, near Nome, in the northwest. Often, he was absent for weeks, and even months, at a time.

Meanwhile, on the homestead with the seven of us, Mom was hard-pressed at times to keep the peace. Our sparsely populated community was spread out over several miles, making interaction with neighbors a relatively rare occurrence. Outside of school and church activities and a Friday night movie at the community hall, Anchor Point offered little for youngsters in the way of occupation or even entertainment.

As is the way with siblings, when boredom set in, excitement was often generated by picking on each other. I'm thankful to report that we all made it to adulthood on amicable terms—and without doing each other any lasting injury—but there were times I'm sure our mother despaired of that happy outcome.

During Dad's visits home, he and Mom began discussing options for occupying the boys' time. Winters were pretty well filled; the high school they attended was in Ninilchik—a twenty-mile, hour-long bus ride away. Busing, school, homework and chores kept them fairly busy, though a determined kid can always squeeze in a fight with a sibling if he thinks creatively. Summers posed the major problem; my parents feared that, if they didn't find something constructive for the boys to do, the boys would find their own, less desirable pursuits.

Around the time we moved into the new house, Dad took a job that was relatively close to home, in Kenai, only 80 miles up the road. The long-term project that would eventually pave the entire road from Anchorage to Anchor Point was still many years from completion, meaning those 80 miles were covered with rough gravel. Rather than spend between three and four hours a day beating his car to death on the commute, Dad rented a small trailer in Kenai during the week and came home on weekends. We all viewed this as a definite improvement over his months-long absences. Unfortunately, when it came to dealing with emergencies, making decisions, or refereeing fights, Mom still bore the majority of family burden.

It also left Dad feeling unconnected with the family. He felt trapped between the needs of his wife and kids and the need to make a living. As happens so often when we mortals lose sight of everything except the rock and the hard place, the Lord stepped in with the solution.

On his way home on Friday evenings, Dad often stopped for fuel at a wide spot in the road known as Kasilof. He got to know the kid who ran the gas station, and, while paying for the gas, would chat and scan the handwritten ads tacked up on the walls.

One night, in the fall of 1961, an ad caught his eye: "Set Net Site for Sale - $3,500.00." The owner's name was listed, so

Dad asked the gas station attendant if he knew the guy. The kid said sure; he lived just up the road a piece.

Dad's interest in commercial fishing had been simmering in the back of his mind for years, though he'd had little time to do more than think about it. As he considered the ad, he reflected that a fish site would kill several birds with one stone: he'd get to live out his dream of fishing the briny deep, his kids would have something to keep them occupied through the idle summer months, he'd have a chance to spend some time with his kids before they were grown and out of the house, and— who knew—they might all earn a little money, as well. However, thirty-five hundred dollars was a major investment for a family of nine. He'd have to think about it for a while. He thought, prayed about it, talked it over with Mom, then finally went out and visited the owner of the fish site.

Either the guy was a great salesman or, perhaps, the spirits of some long-forgotten seafaring Norwegian ancestors were calling. Whatever the cause, after that visit, Dad's next stop was at the bank to get a loan for the difference between what he had in the bank and what he needed. For that $3,500 he acquired a basic set-net package: a World War II-vintage 4 x 4 truck, a tumble-down trailer to serve as a bunkhouse, an assortment of kegs to use as buoys, some used gill nets, and the right to soak those nets in the waters of Cook Inlet off a stretch of beach about thirty miles north of Anchor Point.

We gained access to the beach in one of two ways. The first was via a "road" (I use that word in the loosest sense) that led from a gravel pit up near the highway, down a steep bluff to the shore below. Although this bluff road was no more than an eighth of a mile in length, I felt like I aged years each time I had to traverse it. With the truck lurching along in its lowest gear, loose gravel rolling out from under the tires, we crept down the bank. About midway in this short but hair-raising journey, the road appeared to run right off the edge of the cliff. All one could see out the windshield was sand and water a dizzying distance below. At this point, I always feared that the old truck's gears would fail, sending us flying off into space to land in a lifeless heap on the beach. Of course, the road didn't actually end there, but took a sharp turn to the left, leveling out to a slope that downgraded from terrifying to merely scary. After the upper half, this seemed like a cake walk; my heart and stomach returned to their accustomed locations, and we always managed to arrive at the bottom with bodies—if not nerves—intact. From there, it was a mere half-hour or so of rough driving through soft sand and lurking boulders to arrive at our site, some five miles down the beach.

The other option for access brought us closer to the site before coming down the bank, but involved somewhat more physical exertion. After driving on the highway to an area about a half-mile from (but several hundred feet above) the fish site, we parked the car in the yard of an amiable homeowner. A short walk across a field filled with shoulder-high pushki (pronounced "poosh-key," also known as cow parsnip or wild celery) brought us to the bluff. Here the path lay at a steep angle on the side of the cliff, with a rock-filled ravine below. This stretch of trail was short, and the best way to cross it was to run across before losing one's nerve. Jim hated heights and always needed a hand to get across this stretch. Another short section of steep, but relatively wide, trail led to the edge of a drop-off where, tied to a (one hoped) sturdy willow bush was a stout rope. The rope itself snaked down a wet, muddy footpath through a thick patch of willows. At the bottom of that rope hung another rope, which took us to the bottom of the bluff. Once we hit the beach, a quarter-mile march through soft sand and loose rock brought us at last to the beach site.

As youngsters, slithering down the ropes was our favorite part of the trek. For everyone, that is, except Jim. People with Down's syndrome tend to have low muscle tone, meaning his hands lacked the gripping strength necessary for lowering himself on ropes. This, coupled with his fear of heights, made a trip to the fishing site an ordeal that he soon chose to avoid. If given the choice between a visit to the beach and staying home alone, he gladly saw us off at the door.

Nestled at the foot of the bluff, the "cabin" that sheltered us from the frequent, chilling winds and rain was, in a word, rustic. An 8-foot by 20-foot trailer, it appeared to have been squatting there for the better part of the past century. Amenities included an ancient oil burning heater and a small propane cook top for food preparation. A fold-out couch occupied one end of the cramped space, a double bed filled the other, providing the only seating areas, as well as sleeping accommodations for however many persons were present. We lit kerosene lamps when extra light was needed, though the sun itself provided much of our illumination, thanks to the many hours of summer daylight that Alaskans enjoy. A small creek babbling busily down the bluff beside the cabin supplied us with water, and also kept milk and other items chilled to a satisfactory degree. Toilet facilities were located in an outhouse up a steep path behind the trailer.

Out the front windows of our unprepossessing domicile spread a million-dollar view. A gray sand beach stretched down from the bluff till it met the Cook Inlet, a body of water which holds the dubious distinction of generating the second-highest tides in the world (topped only by the Bay of Fundy in Nova Scotia). At low tide, up to a half-mile of sandy expanse lay between us and the water. When the tide came in, the waves might crash a few feet from our door. Thirty miles across these ever-shifting waters rose the snowcapped Chigmit Mountains— part of the Aleutian Range. At least 3 potentially active volcanoes—Redoubt, Iliamna, and St. Augustine—kept watch over us from afar, along with numerous less volatile peaks.

A small pamphlet called a tide book soon became our family's constant companion. Familiarity with tidal movement is critical to successful commercial fishing. When the high, or flood, tide reaches its highest point, it turns and begins to ebb. Six hours later—give or take a few minutes—it swings again, preparing to flood back in once more. Currents on Cook Inlet run strongly, as the water has a long way to go to reach those famous highs and lows. The brief period at the peak of each tide change is called "slack tide," as the current takes a moment to change direction.

In set-net fishing, a rope strung with large corks (cleverly called the cork line), keeps the top of the net afloat, while a lead-filled line holds the bottom in position. The net hangs down like a curtain, causing the unsuspecting salmon — which have nothing on their minds but returning to their home rivers to spawn — to run into the mesh, which is virtually invisible in the murky water. Brightly-colored buoys mark the ends of the nets, enabling the fishermen to locate them in the vast expanse of sea water. Each 165-foot net must lie at least six hundred feet from its nearest neighbor, so our allotment of six nets covered a fair-sized area of liquid real estate.

June of 1962 saw our family divided, with Mom, Dad, Tim, and Robert spending their weeks at the beach site. In the early part of the season, fishing was restricted to two 24-hour periods per week, on Mondays and Fridays. During these openings, the nets had to be checked at least every six hours, around the time of each slack tide. Of course, there wasn't time to get around to all the nets during the few minutes of slack tide, but the less the fishermen had to wrestle the current, the easier their job was.

We had two open skiffs that we used to run out to the nets. The usual fish-picking procedure was to have two people per boat: one in the stern running the motor, and the other in the bow, ready to grab the net. The net grabber's job was to signal to the motor operator when the boat was close enough to the net, then, with one hand clutching the gunwale, hang by his knees over the bow and scoop up the cork line with his free hand. Sometimes, when the weather was rough, with boat and net bouncing in opposite directions, this process took several attempts.

In the days between Monday's and Friday's fishing periods, the crew mended nets, repaired equipment, and caught up on sleep after fishing from midnight to midnight with little or no down time. Back in Anchor Point, Jim, John, Ken, Ron and I took care of the cow, chickens, selling milk and general housekeeping.

On weekends, the fishermen came home, causing a day or two of mayhem as Mom fired up the old wringer washing machine and washed last week's dirty clothes, then fired up the oven and baked next week's bread. My specialty was cookies; I baked quadruple batches of several varieties to be divided between home and beach for the upcoming week. Dad and the older boys took care of any repairs or maintenance that needed attention, to head off possible problems while we younger kids were home alone with no phone or other method of communication with the fishing site.

Our first summer in the commercial fishing business proved an educational experience for the entire family. The fishermen learned what was involved with setting, picking, and mending nets and how to tell the difference between red, king, silver, and humpy salmon — also known as Sockeye, Chinook, Coho and Pink, respectively. The home crew discovered that, even with no one around to prod us, livestock, housework and garden chores still had to be done. Jim kept us on task with the cow chores, but more than once we froze the milk, having forgotten to set the timer on our converted freezer/cooler.

As if the learning curve was not steep enough, that year brought to the inlet the biggest run of pink salmon in history. The Monday/Friday restriction was lifted in mid-July, and fishing continued all week long, around the clock. Mom bore the added concern of the five of us back on the homestead with no way to stay in contact. She burned up the thirty-mile stretch of road between Kasilof and Anchor Point, checking on us, picking up supplies, and heading back down to the fish camp. Dad, Tim, and Robert grabbed meals and naps in between high and low tides, at which times they had to be out picking fish. By the time the run finally petered out in August, the fishing crew was exhausted and ready to put the nets away till next season.

The excessive blessing we received that year in pink salmon enabled Dad to pay off the loan, with enough left over to convince him the whole experience was worth tackling again the following year. Though the division of labor changed from year to year as Tim, Robert, and John moved on to higher education and the military, the fish site remained a family business each summer for nearly a decade.

As the summers marched by, Jim increasingly became the anchor of the home crew. He cared not at all for boats and schedules that shifted with the tides. He much preferred his cow and chickens, whose schedules stayed constant the year around. Sometimes Mom found it necessary to leave him in charge of the home scene, the rest of us being required to help on the fish site. Jim accepted the responsibility gladly; he knew how and when to milk the cow and could take care of the other necessary chores on a short-term basis, and probably preferred that we be out of his way.

An experience Jim endured a year or two after we began the commercial fishing venture probably quenched any budding interest he might have harbored in the maritime life before it could blossom. We non-fishing members of the family occasionally took turns visiting the site for a few days. I suspect that my dad, in addition to furnishing a treat to the homebound kids, hoped that we would be bitten by the same fishing bug that had infected him. A crop of enthusiastic young fisher persons would ensure a continuing supply of ready hands as my older brothers eyed, and eventually left for, more distant shores.

As mentioned previously, the nets were intended to hang vertically in the water, crosswise to the current. Each end was tied to a brightly colored buoy which helped locate the nets, as well as keep them in place. As the salmon swam unsuspectingly up the inlet, they would run into this invisible curtain and become entangled.

Sometimes, due to rough weather or careless tying of the net to the buoy, one end of the net became detached. The loose end of the net then swung into the current and flapped uselessly, parallel to the swimming fish. This was called "flagging." A flagged net called for immediate attention in order to return it to proper functioning position.

On the day in question, Jim was on his first extended visit to the beach. At high tide, the crew headed out to pick the fish from the nets. Jim accompanied my dad and John in one of the boats, while Tim and Robert operated the other. Someone spotted a flagged net, causing everyone to kick into emergency mode. Initial reconnaissance of the situation revealed that it would take all four crew members working out of one boat to rectify the problem, but that left no room for Jim. They knew, with the four of them slithering around, wrestling a net in a pitching skiff, there was no safe place from which Jim could observe. Dad decided the safest option was for Jim to wait in the spare boat until the operation was completed.

He explained to Jim briefly what the plan was, then tied his temporary haven securely to a buoy on the end of a properly-functioning net. Scrambling into the boat with his other sons, he set off in pursuit of the flagged unit. A slight breeze created choppiness on the water's surface, which caused the boat to bounce around in a way that a newcomer to the experience would find disconcerting, if not downright terrifying. The dipping and swaying motion meant nothing to the seasoned crew, but it was a totally new and not particularly pleasant experience for stability-loving Jim.

He crouched in the bottom of the boat, hands gripping the gunwale as he watched the skiff bear his dad and brothers away. Soon they disappeared from sight, leaving him in a rocking, lurching boat—so unlike the comfortingly solid earth he knew. Everything was strange; it was hard to move in the hip boots, chest waders, and rain coat that make up the fisherman's standard gear, but that was okay with him, since he wasn't about to move, anyway, for fear of rocking the boat and causing it to overturn. The skiff was a fairly seaworthy vessel, but Jim was no judge of ocean craft. For all he knew, a hiccup could send him headlong into the cold, unfriendly depths. He didn't even have his watch, which would at least help occupy his mind while he huddled out there all alone. Watches tended to go on strike when repeatedly plunged into icy salt water, so they remained on shore, in the cabin.

A swell slightly larger than its predecessors lifted the boat, causing Jim's stomach to lurch. He whimpered with fear and hunkered down even further into the bottom of the boat. The mountains rising majestically across the inlet may be the stuff of picture postcards, but Jim had no interest in their impersonal beauty; his eyes strained for a glimpse of the small skiff with four guys who could rescue him from that miserably rolling ocean.

Less than fifteen minutes later, the fishermen returned. Dad felt his conscience jabbing at him as he took in Jim's tear-filled eyes and frightened look. Since he enjoyed the boating experience himself, it didn't occur to him that merely waiting in the boat would be so traumatic for Jim. Quickly he hopped into Jim's skiff, and turned it shoreward. Once safely on the beach, he asked, "Were you scared?"

Honest as always, Jim replied, "Yeah, I cry a li' bit."

Whether or not this experience played a large role in Jim's lack of interest in the fishing site remains unknown, but I'm sure it didn't make him any fonder of the sea.

In the early '70s, Dad sold the beach site and purchased a drift-fishing boat, which meant the entire process—fishing, eating, sleeping and everything else—took place far out on the inlet. When Jim realized that his feet might not touch land from one day to the next, he flatly refused to have anything to do with it. He'd stay home, thank you very much, and leave the seafaring to the foolhardy.

Games and Buddies

Put your hands together, Jim!" Ronny yelled. The soft ball he'd just tossed zoomed with uncanny accuracy toward the opening between Jim's outstretched hands.

"Ow-w-w-!" came the inevitable cry, as the ball found its usual target in the middle of Jim's face. Ronny winced: that had to hurt—again.

With the rest of us growing older and becoming busy with our own concerns, Ronny—the youngest—turned for companionship to the one who still loved a good game of cops and robbers or cowboys and Indians. Together, they made the surrounding woods ring with the sounds of bullets, cars, or whatever the game du jour demanded.

On this day it was a simple game of catch. After a few tosses, Ronny discovered that Jim, despite all the willingness in the world, didn't know how to catch a ball.

It soon became obvious that Jim wasn't going to learn this all in one step. Ronny decided to break it down into smaller pieces.

Standing almost close enough to touch each other's outstretched hands, Ronny demonstrated how Jim should hold his mitt to catch the ball in the pocket. He lobbed a soft underhand pitch directly into the mitt.

"I got it!" Jim exclaimed, delighted.

"That's the way," Ronny encouraged, "Now let's take a step back." He lobbed it again from a little farther away. Jim scooped his mitt at the ball, but missed.

"That's okay; let's try again." Ronny fetched the ball, and tossed it carefully back to Jim. Success! Jim dug the ball out of the mitt and tossed it to Ronny.

Back and forth flew the ball. Sometimes Jim caught it; many times he missed. After some sessions when the ball appeared to be purposely avoiding Jim's reaching hand, Ronny expected him to toss his mitt and swear off ball games forever, but he never did. He wanted to play; he was determined to play.

Little by little, Jim's skill increased. Once he could catch underhand pitches easily, his youthful instructor moved on to gentle overhand throws. Gradually Jim got the hang of how to hold his mitt so his face was protected while keeping an eye on the ball.

After weeks of practice, Ronny's patient teaching was rewarded. Jim was able to catch not only a ball thrown to him, but a batted one, as well. Ronny got a workout during Jim's turns at bat, since his only concern was to connect with the ball in such a way that it went far. North, south, east, west, or straight up: as long as it went a long way, Jim considered it a successful hit.

As school consumed more and more of his siblings' time, Jim was left to generate his own amusements. Of course he had chores to fill some of his time, but he still had many hours on his hands with no companions. As with so many difficulties in his life, he solved the problem in his own way: he invented his own companions.

Maybe he was influenced by all the make-believe he participated in with us when we were younger; maybe he spent too much time listening to John and Ken, who are wicked mimics. However it happened, he developed a group of fantasy friends who kept him entertained and busy any time he was at loose ends.

Chief among these "buddies" was "Smajer." I heard him addressing Smajer by name for some time before I understood where the moniker came from. We often reversed each other's names, so that Tim became "Mit," and so on. Instead of calling Jim "Mij," we reversed his given name, James and called him "Smaje." Jim tacked on an extra letter and created a whole new person. Some of his other buddies were based on people he knew. I often heard our preacher's deep bass voice calling his wife, and the reply in her sweet Southern drawl, when neither of them was anywhere around. Other participants were sports heroes or characters he had encountered on radio or TV; the rest—as far as we could tell—were figments of Jim's own fertile fancy.

When he got caught up in his make-believe world, he would forget that we could overhear, and silliness would reign. He'd have a number of different people carrying on conversations, changing from voice to voice with a rapidity and ease that astounded us. Sometimes the buddies would argue; other times they'd sing. Whatever they did, they usually left him giggling over something one of them said.

If anyone walked into the room, he clammed up, seeming not to realize that we could hear every word from any corner of the house. He would sit with a rather pained look on his face, obviously waiting for us to get lost. Once we removed our intrusive presence, he picked up right where he left off.

After listening to a baseball, basketball or football game on the radio, he and the buddies would head outside and down the driveway for the victory parade. Usually our first indication that the parade had started was the sound of drums (all sound effects were made with his own lips, tongue, and vocal chords—no real instruments were harmed in the production of these musical melees.) Soon we would hear the bugles playing a sort of "James Lionel Sousa" thing, with a TA-TA-TA and a few crashes of cymbals. Interspersed with the marches, he would sing a rousing hymn or throw in a patriotic number. "The Battle Hymn of the Republic" was a favorite, especially the "Glory, glory halleluia" part.

Before long, he would come into view, marching up the driveway with one hand in the air, apparently to direct the rest of the band. Depending on the level of satisfaction he felt at the outcome of the game, he might bring the marchers to a halt when they reached the yard or continue on down the woodlot trail. Finally, he brought the whole thing back to the yard for the grand finale. This usually consisted of the parade standing at attention while several more pieces were performed. These could range from "When the Roll is Called Up Yonder" to "O Come All Ye Faithful." When he deemed the time right, he led the entire group in a round of applause, and the parade was over.

Jim was nothing if not versatile. He loved to play basketball, and we had a hoop set up outside which received much attention from all of us over the years. It received a special workout from Jim. He started out as the player, then switched to cheerleader, whooping and hollering after every basket. When he perceived an infraction of a rule, he stepped effortlessly into the role of referee, castigating the errant player thoroughly before allowing the play to continue. Finally, he sounded the buzzer to end the game. There was one great advantage to this sort of play: he never lost.

Jim also reenacted real-life scenes, with his own special twist. I remember watching him coming up the woodlot trail dragging a gunny sack, every line of his body proclaiming that this was a load almost too heavy for him to manage. On closer inspection, I realized the sack was empty. I asked him what he was doing.

"Bossy had a calf," came the reply.

I puzzled over this response for a long time. Finally, as I watched him manipulate the gunny sack, I realized how his mind was working.

When our cows had calves, we were not allowed in the barn, my folks being of the opinion that the miracle of birth was no business of ours. By the time we saw the calf it was born, up on its feet, and receiving a bath from its mamma's tongue and a good rubbing with a gunny sack from Dad. Jim put the facts, as he knew them, together, and decided that the calf was dropped off by some mysterious entity down in the woodlot (possibly an extraordinarily muscular stork?). Dad picked it up there, brought it up to the barn in a gunny sack, and presented it to the expectant cow.

His make-believe calves eventually made up a considerable herd of nonexistent cattle; in fact, he bragged that he owned "a sousand" (thousand). As my friend Carol discovered, those cows were as real to Jim as we were. Carol lived a mile up the North Fork Road from us, making her one of our nearest neighbors. She and I spent countless hours rambling the road between our homes, engrossed in nonstop chatter as little girls love to do. Often, as we approached our house, our concentration was broken by the sight of Jim hustling toward us with his hand outstretched and an authoritative order to "Stop!" The first time this happened Carol stood, mystified, with me in our appointed place, watching as he ran from one side of the driveway to the other, making shooing motions, all the while keeping an eye on us to make sure we stayed put. Finally unable to contain her curiosity, she asked, "Whacha doin', Jim?"

He replied matter-of-factly, "Gettin' the cows off the road." He was not about to have any injuries—real or imagined— caused by his livestock, even if they existed only in his vivid imagination.

The family got so used to his games that we sometimes shrugged off things he said to us, thinking he was in his fantasy world when in fact he was in dead earnest. We only found out later, when Jim decided that we were not moving in the direction he wanted, and took matters into his own hands.

The Piano

It was a raw October afternoon in 1963. Through the large, square picture window on the north side of our house, gray skies threatened snow. Daylight was becoming a precious commodity, as the sun set five minutes earlier each day. Though it wasn't yet four-thirty, we had long since flipped on the overhead fluorescent lights to chase the gloom back outside where it belonged.

Inside the house, Mary Epperson was in her element. She tapped toes that barely reached the floor. She wagged her head till I felt dizzy watching her. She bounced on the stool, while her fingers flew across the keys of the old upright piano in a lively rendition of a ragtime ditty.

This little lady was the reason our house held a piano. The year before, she had put out the word that she had an extra piano that needed a temporary home—and that she'd make a deal on piano lessons for the foster family. My mother jumped at the opportunity.

Mary, or Mrs. Epperson as we youngsters respectfully called her, had just finished four grueling hours of piano lessons. This was a weekly ritual, as she patiently nudged the four youngest Haakensons toward greater proficiency on the keyboard. For 240 minutes, to four different sets of ears she had repeated such phrases as, "That's good, dear. Now—just once more" and "Very nice; just one more time" and "Let's try this section again."

It couldn't be easy to maintain that patience as she guided pair after pair of hands with their stumbling fingers, but I never knew her to lose that cool, or to be less than positive in her dealings with any of us. After the lessons were over was her fun time, when she let loose and played a few songs, probably with the secret hope that she would instill a sense of music appreciation into our left-brained, homestead-bound souls.

In my twelve-year-old eyes, Mrs. Epperson was surely one of the great pianists of the world. She was a short, slender lady with short, dark, curly hair, and small, dainty hands—hands that were presently making some very big sounds come forth from the piano. She always said she admired my hands with their long fingers. I thought she was being kind; though I could reach several more notes than she could, mine too often seemed to be the wrong ones. If she hit any wrong notes, I rarely noticed them.

From my listening post beside the piano I could observe John, the brother next up the line in age from me—the eldest of the budding pianists. He sat with a politely listening look on his face, but he had told me what he planned to do with a piano once he was grown. Somewhere he had read that the record for stuffing an entire piano (in pieces, of course) through a 12-inch hole stood at nine and a half minutes. He intended, when he got enough money to buy his own piano, to better that record by several minutes.

My younger brothers, Ken and Ron, loitered nearby, doing their best to appear unimpressed by Mrs. E's performance. These two—the worst pair of scamps I ever hoped to see—spent most of their waking moments criticizing or making fun of everybody they knew. As Mrs. Epperson played on, I intercepted a smirking glance between them and knew exactly what that look meant: "Yeah, she can play, but she ruins it with all that Emotion." The two of them waged a continual, vigilant battle against any sign of such uncool behavior, especially from a family member. It's not that they had anything against "emotion" in general, but they didn't approve of mixing it with music. That smacked too much of "showing off."

I thought back to a recent practice session in which I had allowed my body to sway ever-so-slightly as I reached for an octave at the far bass end of the keyboard. I didn't know I was being watched till Ken appeared at my elbow like an evil genie.

"You look stupid," he pronounced. "What're you tryin' to do, be Mrs. Epperson?" After that, even if I could waggle my head and bounce my rump around while I played without losing my place, I wouldn't, for fear of being accused of showing off or looking stupid.

Finishing the ragtime piece, Mrs. Epperson moved on to "Autumn Leaves." She carried the melody on the bass with a mellow legato, while her right hand tumbled down the treble keys, simulating the falling leaves. She swayed her body first to the left to introduce a phrase of melody, then bowed her head to the right as she concentrated on the intricate fingering required of her right hand. We listened in (mostly) respectful silence, punctuated by the occasional snickering snort from the anti-emotion element, though they were quickly quelled by a glare from Mom.

"Autumn Leaves" reached its gentle, almost dreamy conclusion, and Mrs. Epperson arose from the piano. She headed over to the kitchen, her stockinged feet padding softly over the polished hardwood floor. It had become her custom to drink a cup of tea with our mother after our lessons were over. Perhaps she needed the pick-me-up to recover from the last four hours. Or perhaps she just wanted to relax a few moments before starting her drive to the Epperson ranch, some ten neck-jarring miles up the road from us.

As she seated herself, she was greeted by Jim, who was diligently dunking a tea bag into a cup of steaming water. His face, with its small, slanted eyes and overlarge lips so typical of one with Down's syndrome, crinkled in a welcoming smile. He motioned toward the brewing tea.

"Not too squong," he stated. His thickened tongue made speech difficult, but he wanted Mrs. E to know that he remembered she once said she didn't like her tea too strong. That being the case—and in the interest of frugality—he decided that she and Mom should share a tea bag. Carefully he transferred the bag to Mom's cup.

"Oh, Jim," Mom reproved, embarrassed, "Mrs. Epperson can have her own tea bag."

"No, no," Mrs. E protested, laughing. "This is just the way I like it."

At this point, we kids lost interest in what was happening in the kitchen. John prowled off to hole up in his room, probably to plot further destruction of his future piano. I flopped my gawky frame onto the battered naugahyde couch in the living room and picked up my latest library book, a *Hardy Boys* mystery. I adjusted my glasses and soon lost myself in the story, barely aware of Mom and Mrs. E chatting in the kitchen and Ken and Ron somewhere nearby, alternately giggling and squabbling as they set up a board game.

Suddenly, a new sound chimed forth: a bass of mellow legato, followed by a tumble of notes from the treble. The tune was missing, but the pattern was recognizable. This was unusual enough to cause me to put my book down. Even Ken and Ron perked up their ears. We were used to Jim's habit of imitating our singing, actions and even voices, but this was the first time we had heard him attempt the piano. Mom was the only one who appeared unsurprised to see Jim at the keyboard.

(Later she told me that, during the day while the rest of us were in school, he often amused himself at the piano.) We looked toward the piano and saw Mrs. Epperson standing transfixed, watching Jim give a creditable imitation of her recent efforts.

Jim was no savant, but he was a pretty good mimic. Seated on the piano bench, his squat body bore little resemblance to Mrs. Epperson's trim form, but he imitated her mannerisms to a T. He leaned to the left, plunking out a few notes with the emotion, if not the melody, achieved by Mrs. Epperson. He then swayed right, lowering his head till his nose nearly touched the keys. His stiff, untrained fingers lacked Mrs. E's agility, but did their best to duplicate her difficult chromatics and arpeggios.

I sneaked a peek at our piano teacher. How would she react to this obvious—though innocent—mimicry of her performance? Would she be offended, thinking Jim was doing this maliciously? I knew Jim was incapable of malice, but it was hard to predict how someone outside the family would interpret some of the things he did.

Would she laugh at him? I hoped not. We had never received a full explanation of why Jim was the way he was, but we knew him well enough to know he couldn't help it. We might occasionally laugh or tease Jim over something he did, in the cruel way of siblings, but my hackles rose at the thought of someone else having a laugh at his expense.

What happened next confirmed that Mrs. Epperson was the classy lady I had always considered her to be. I saw the gleam of moisture in her dark eyes. She seemed stunned by Jim's interest in the piano. I could almost see her revising her opinion of his abilities. I would bet the thought uppermost in her mind was that he should be the one taking lessons.

As the impromptu performance concluded, Mrs. E reached out to grasp Jim by the shoulders. "That was wonderful," she enthused. Jim beamed proudly. Here was one Haakenson who didn't at all mind being the center of attention.

She continued to stand, smiling at him. And again, I suspected she would love to ditch the four of us, and concentrate on the one who felt the music, and was not afraid to show Emotion. Finally, smile fading, she looked over at Mom. With regret thick in her voice she murmured, "If only...if only..." She didn't finish the sentence, but the words hung there unspoken: if only Jim didn't have Down's syndrome.

90

Pinochle and Other Games

Twenty-five year-old Jim sat at his mother's elbow, studying the cards she held spread, fanlike, in her hand. At least once a week she and Lionel got together with their good friends, Ted and Ruth Rozak, to play a few games of pinochle. Customarily, Esther and Ruth squared off against Ted and Lionel. Jim was "pullin' for the womans," as usual; being a true gentleman, he rooted for the women to win.

Throughout the game, from the first bid proffered to the last trick taken, he remained absorbed by the play, whooping when the "womans" made a good move, moaning in sympathy if the guys got the upper hand. From time to time he circulated around the table, checking the other players' hands, knowing better than to make revealing comments, but unable to prevent the occasional exuberant hoot, though he left it up to the competitors to interpret these expressions as they pleased.

Over the course of several years, Jim observed hundreds of such games. Not only did the adults play, but his siblings had all become fairly proficient at pinochle. Our parents saw the game not only as a way to practice math skills, but as a channel for turning our worse inclinations for amusement on long winter evenings into a friendlier form of rivalry. As we got older, they saw our tendency to shut down and crawl off into our rooms, thereby avoiding interaction with the family. They hoped that, if what was happening around the kitchen table sounded like more fun than sitting in solitary splendor in one's bedroom, perhaps the "generation gap" (a phrase just coming into vogue), would be minimized. So pinochle, Monopoly, Sorry, and other board and card games became our motivation to get homework and chores done as quickly as possible, so as to have the maximum time to play before bedtime.

Jim remained on the fringes of such play no longer than was necessary to learn the basic principles of the games, first mastering the mysteries of the board game "Sorry." This is a fairly simple game, though many cards have specific instructions. For example, a card bearing a "1" or a "2" must be drawn in order to move one's playing piece, or marker, from the "Start" circle; a "2" can be used to go two spaces forward or backward, and a "4" means you must go backward four spaces. A card bearing the word "Sorry" gives the holder the right to knock another player's marker off the board and back to "Start." This bit of sabotage is generally accompanied by an unabashedly hypocritical "Sorry!" from the perpetrator.

Since he was unable to read, Jim used us to remind him of the rules until he had them all memorized. He eventually became so proficient that he made many of his moves without bothering to count the spaces. When his marker was the unlucky target of an opponent's "Sorry" card, he fumed silently, his face plainly proclaiming his displeasure with this state of affairs. On the flip side, he was not above gloating when he managed to knock one of us off the board.

Pinochle was his ultimate goal in the games department. He longed to master that game. Eventually, he began sitting in on our games, with one of us coaching him through the various intricacies of play, slowly increasing his skill to the point that he was able to play his own hand.

Over the course of about six years, he went from playing with four players and a single deck of cards to double-deck games with either four or six players. The most indulgent of observers could never consider him a brilliant player, but he acquitted himself adequately. He and his partners even won at times, whether because of, or in spite of, some rather rash playing remaining an unanswered question.

After holiday meals, when everyone was so full they wanted nothing more than to sit and suffer the effects of too much of a good thing, Jim began bustling around, clearing the table. One's first thought was, "Wow, what a helpful guy. How nice it would be if the other males would do as much." At this point, the women usually pitched in with the washing and general cleanup.

Once the table was bare, Jim's ulterior motive became clear, as he arranged chairs and set out decks of cards. He wanted a pinochle game. Who could resist that hopeful face and coaxing grin? In case we didn't get the hint, he picked up a deck of cards and shuffled and reshuffled it, keeping at it until a foursome or six-some assembled around him.

Though he never verbalized it in quite this way, "practice makes perfect" was an axiom that Jim believed in and acted upon. For him, lack of partners never prevented a rousing game of pinochle from happening. Seating himself at the table, he dealt out four piles of cards, with some of his best "buddies" rounding out the group. (One time, I inadvertently sat down at the table during one of these games; Jim was as offended as if I had deliberately parked myself on the buddy's lap.) They, of course, needed his assistance, so he turned their cards over and played all the hands, each as if it were his own. Considering the fact that they were invisible, those buddies managed to make a good bit of trouble, judging by the yelling and arguing that took place. In the end, Jim managed to soothe everyone's ruffled feelings, and still won all games.

Lionel and Esther Haakenson with their children outside the homestead cabin in Anchor Point. 1958. Jim is in the middle of the second row. To his right is Robert, to the left, Tim. Mary is directly in front of Robert. Standing in front of Jim and Tim is John. In the front row are Ron, the youngest, and Ken.

Right, the boys display their catch of the day. Left to right are John, Jim, Kenny, Robert, and cousin Bill Dixson.

Left, Lionel and Esther Haakenson examine Daisy, the family's last cow. Jim is standing behind Daisy. 1967.

Below, coming into the house after finishing milking the cow, one of the jobs Jim made his own. He took it seriously, and never wanted to be late.

Above, Jim's "rig", his three-wheel ATV, was one of his proudest possessions.

Fishing was one of the highlights of Jim's life. Above, he displays a salmon caught at Silver Salmon Creek. Right, his catch of the day was a midsize halibut.

A Job

By 1970, Tim, Robert, and John had graduated from high school and gone off to military duty. I returned from my first year of college and worked for the summer on the fishing site with Dad, Ken, and Ron. Jim—now barnyard baron—had taken full charge of the cow and chickens.

Our conversations often revolved around getting jobs, as we wrestled, as all teens do, with the question of what we wanted to do with our lives. (Though a teaching degree in special education was my long-term goal, I needed some sort of interim employment that would help me accumulate enough money to attend several more years of college.)

Jim never wanted to be left out of the action, so as words like "jobs" and "work" began circulating, he also started talking about a job; in fact, many of his "buddy games" began to be played out as if he were already employed. He lugged fantasy fish nets one day, the next he might be out on the driveway with a couple of flashlights, directing airplanes to safety on a runway of his mind's devising. None of us thought there was any chance of actually finding a job for Jim in our area. We had never heard of the sheltered workshops which provide employment for the disabled, and, at that time, knew of no local resources to which we could turn, so we brushed off his attempts to talk about it. We hoped his livestock chores and the jobs he did around the house would be enough to keep him content. We should have known better.

Throughout the 1969-'70 school year Ken–then a senior–participated in a training program for teens that had him working with our old friend Uncle Bert, who was custodian at the Anchor Point grade school. Ken would come home full of stories about the fun he had working with Uncle Bert. Soon, Jim's games and conversation began to revolve around getting a job with Bert.

The following school year, as Jim walked out the driveway with Ronny to see him off to school, he would catch a glimpse of Bert's house through the trees and say, "I'm gonna get a job from Bert." Day after day, he said it. Ronny took little notice, viewing it, as we all did, as another of Jim's fantasy games. Little did we realize how serious he was.

One spring day in 1971, Jim appeared and began to tell everyone in sight, "I got a job...Uncle Bert gave me a job." We still believed a job for Jim was an impossibility, so we again failed to take him seriously.

Lo and behold, a short time later Bert flamed into the yard, all atremble with excitement. Jim had taken upon himself that which the rest of us thought impossible: he had gone down to Bert's place and asked for a job.

My parents and Bert talked for a long time; he was sure there was a place at the school for Jim. He explained that, at least for a while, he would have to work as an unpaid volunteer, since there was no precedent for hiring someone with Jim's challenges. Dad and Mom did not care about that; they knew Jim would gladly pay the school, if only he could work. As summer was almost upon us, Bert and my parents spent the next months writing to everyone who might know anything about getting Jim a position. Bert promised that, even if nothing official came through, he would let Jim come down to the school as a volunteer.

By fall, the state gave the okay for Jim to begin, and he proudly started his job. He got himself up and dressed each morning, ate the breakfast Mom prepared for him, strutted down the driveway and, through a special arrangement with the school district, fulfilled another dream: he rode the school bus to work.

It would have been hard to find a job for which Jim was better suited. Under Bert's tutelage he learned the right way to collect trash, sweep and mop floors, and scrub sinks, desks and walls. He worked in the lunchroom, running errands for the cook, setting up the tables, and cleaning up after the lunch period was over. During the winter months, he shoveled the walkways, keeping them clear of snow and ice. He also served diligently as the self-appointed behavior police, remonstrating any children he saw running in the halls, horsing around, or doing anything else he considered inappropriate school conduct.

Unlike the grump who had refused an education to Jim years earlier, this principal, John Jones, was one of his leading supporters. Between them, he and the school secretary did all they could to smooth Jim's transition to the world of work. They made it their mission to keep my folks informed of what was happening at school, especially any changes in routine that required some action on Jim's part. He brought goodies when the staff had get-togethers, money for special fund-raisers, and cans of coffee when the stock in the custodians' room got low.

And every day, without fail, he brought a zeal and enthusiasm for his job that impressed and inspired students, staff and community members alike.

The state did not seem to know how to handle Jim's compensation, so he received no pay for many months, but my parents felt that the experience he was getting was priceless. He was busy and happy, which was payment enough for the time.

At the end of that school year, Bert reluctantly informed Jim and my folks that the training program only allowed Jim to work at the Anchor Point school for one year. All was not lost, though: he thought there was a chance for Jim to work in Homer, a larger town about sixteen miles away, where many of Anchor Point's kids attended high school. The head custodian at the junior high school there was a fellow homesteader from Anchor Point who had watched Jim grow up. This man was willing to transport Jim to school and oversee his work, then he could come home on the bus that carried the high school students in the afternoon. My parents, feeling that the experience was worth the lack of pay, allowed him to commute to Homer each day.

For a few months of his time in Homer, Jim again worked for the experience. Around December, some funding became available for a small stipend, allowing him to bring home a paycheck. He proudly showed his check to anyone who visited the house, but its value in his eyes was nothing compared to the honor of being allowed to work. He would walk up to strangers at church, shake hands and say, "Hi! I'm Jim; I got a job." Having thus established a relationship, he would rattle on, telling them when, where, and with whom he worked. The work he did at the Homer school was similar to what he had done in Anchor Point, so he was able to use and sharpen the skills he had learned from Bert.

In the spring of 1973, as Jim neared the end of his second year of work, my parents knew they had to make sure that there would be a job for Jim again in the fall. He would never have given them any peace otherwise. The Homer school offered some encouraging news, saying that they had gotten some funding, and would be able to continue paying Jim the same amount he had received the year before. Though the money did not matter, it was nice to know that they were willing to pay him, and the commute to Homer seemed a small sacrifice in order to allow him to continue working.

Then, shortly after the start of school that fall, Mr. Jones, the principal from Anchor Point, showed up at my folks' house (they still didn't have a phone). He told them that Anchor Point wanted Jim back. At the time there was no money, but if Jim was willing to work for a hot lunch from the cafeteria at noon, Mr. Jones was pretty sure there would be funding for his position soon. My folks thought it over and decided that eliminating the drive to Homer was worth it, since the job was never about the money, anyway. Accordingly, Jim started back to work in Anchor Point. In a few months, the funding did come through, and Jim again had a check to show off. Those first checks were little more than a pittance, but Jim did not care; he had a job!

As time went on, Jim became ever more a part of the school scene. In addition to his day job, he attended evening activities, so he could help clean up. Although cleanup did not officially start until the function was over, he bustled around all evening, making sure trash was picked up, chairs were straight, and kids were not getting rowdy.

When my parents chose not to attend an evening school function, they would drop Jim off at the school and go home, knowing that some accommodating neighbor would deliver him safely afterwards. Thanks to our community's small size, everyone knew Jim and looked out for him. And, as at least one person discovered, Jim sometimes returned the favor.

After an evening sports event, Ann, a good friend and one of our nearest neighbors, was driving home with her two young children. Up ahead, she spied Jim's familiar figure walking, with his distinctive side-to-side gait, along the side of the road, headed home. She took her foot off the accelerator, planning to offer him a ride, but as she stepped on the brake she felt no response. She coasted to a stop beside him. The car was nearly to the curve at the top of the hill leading down to the river. The hill was not particularly long or steep, but a coasting car could gain a good bit of momentum by the time it reached the bridge at the bottom. In a split second Ann saw in her mind's eye the car with its helpless occupants hurtling down the now-precipitously steep cliff, and herself frantically attempting to guide the rocketing vehicle across a bridge that in her imagination had shrunk to the size of a footpath.

As Jim climbed into the car Ann put her trepidation into words: "Jim, I don't have any brakes!"

Jim, with calm good sense, replied, "Put it in first gear. You be fine." Ann, feeling rather foolish for not thinking of it herself, shifted into low gear and crept down the not-so-steep hill and across the bridge, which miraculously expanded back to its normal width. She glanced over at Jim, who was placidly unaware of the reassurance afforded by his practical words. At my parents' house, he got out of the car with his usual, "Thanks for the ride." He didn't quite understand Ann's response, "No—thank *you!*" Ann knew she would never look at Jim quite the same: he may have mental challenges, but he had a practical gift for problem-solving that was impressive in its simplicity.

He had always enjoyed baseball and basketball as played by the family in the yard. A favorite evening pastime was listening to games on the radio and—in later years—television. With his job, he got to participate in a whole new way: live, at the games. He never missed a home game, and even accompanied the team on the bus to games in nearby towns. When that happened, he would have to take enough money to cover expenses for meals. The secretary told Mom approximately how much he would need, and Mom put the necessary amount in his wallet. The coaches and students helped him order and pay for his food. This was a new experience for Jim, since we rarely went to restaurants, and when we did, one of us put in his order for him.

For the most part, the students accepted Jim and even looked out for him. A few students teased him, but they were the exception. One woman, when she found out her two boys were making Jim's life miserable, made them come out to the house and apologize to my parents in person for persecuting him.

If possible, Jim loved the school atmosphere even more at Christmas. He would stand inside the classrooms and listen while the kids rehearsed carols for the Christmas program. This was much too good to leave at school. In his imagination he brought the classes, songs, instruments and audience all home for a command performance.

He truly was a one-man band. As conductor, he selected and led the songs, keeping time with a ruler transformed by imagination into a baton. He played the part of the singers, belting out the words with a total lack of inhibition. As disciplinarian, he would stop himself in mid-word to snap his fingers at or verbally reprove a goof-off in the choir. After the song, he became the audience, clapping and cheering with wholehearted appreciation.

We watched Jim blossom in his job. He could not express it verbally, but he clearly showed the feeling of self-worth he gained by being a contributing member of the community. He smiled more, conversed more easily, and became more outgoing toward people outside of our family. He soon knew, and was known by, almost everyone in our community, even reaching minor celebrity status thanks to several articles published in local papers which highlighted his devotion to his job.

His eagerness to serve shone through, as he began adding little tasks where he perceived a need. One of these managed to cause a certain teacher considerable mental anxiety before she figured out the solution to the Great Calendar Mystery.

Betha, like many other teachers, had a daily desk calendar, the kind that has a separate page for each day. Shortly after the start of the school year, she reached for her calendar one morning to change the date. "That's funny," she thought, "It's already changed. I don't remember flipping the page last night. Oh, well, I guess I've got too much on my mind."

The next morning, it happened again: the page was turned to the new date when she went to change it. Once again, she figured she had done it without thinking. This went on for several weeks. Every morning Betha puzzled over that turned calendar page, and resolved to pay attention to the moment she flipped it. How could she be doing this so consistently, and have no recollection of it?

One day after school as she worked at her desk, another teacher stopped by her room. As they chatted, Jim bustled in with the trash cart to empty her waste baskets. When he finished, just before he left the room, he reached over and flipped the page of her calendar. End of mystery. Betha was relieved to know that she wasn't losing her mind. (If she had known what we did about Jim's obsession with calendars, this would have come as no surprise at all.)

Jim continued working under the state-sponsored training program for several years; then in 1976 he became an employee of the school district. Soon, his life became too busy to support both his school job and the cow chores. There was no question which avenue he would choose; he bid a final farewell to Daisy and she moved on to other pastures, leaving him to concentrate his energies in his chosen field.

Jim At Work

A-*way on a craw wee toe!*" Jim informed the surrounding flora and fauna loudly and confidently, if somewhat obscurely. On a crisp, sunny spring morning, he was headed to work, just as he had been doing for several years now. He skirted clumps of rotting snow, ice covered mud puddles, and frost boils with the ease of long practice. Meanwhile he whiled away the morning amble down the driveway with his inimitable rendition of one of his favorite hymns, "The Way of the Cross Leads Home." He shifted into falsetto for the second phrase of the chorus, then suddenly dropped to a normal speaking voice: "Watch it, sir. You stay over there." His gaze was fastened on a big cow moose and her yearling calf munching willow twigs in the woods just off the driveway.

His morning walks to the bus frequently included moose sightings, since the animals range freely throughout the area. In general, moose are shy, preferring their own company to that of other species, though they manage to run afoul of humans on a fairly regular basis. Almost every resident cherishes a favorite story regarding one of these huge herbivores. Their tales depict a variety of moose miscreants, from the furtive — who clean out broccoli patches in the dead of night — to the bold — who barge onto porches, and even into homes and public buildings, seeking food.

Spring is an especially fragile time for the moose temperament. Any one of a number of conditions can cause a moose to temporarily shed its mild-mannered disposition and go on a rampage. The animals are ravenously hungry after a long hard winter with limited browse, and starvation never improves anyone's temper. Also, new calves are born in May and June, making the cows, like all good mothers, extra protective. Dogs, wolves, bears, humans, cars–all cause an untold amount of stress to moose. Locals know the best and safest policy is to give them a wide berth at any time of the year.

On this occasion, Jim's four-legged audience appeared unimpressed with the lone human songster. Very probably, if these two spent any time in the woods near our property, they were well-acquainted with this noisy, but non-threatening individual. Or perhaps they weren't overly severe music critics. In any case, they didn't seem put out by either Jim's presence or performance. He continued on his unhurried way, only his

watchful eyes and palm-out hand signal indicating his awareness of potential danger. Another dozen paces took him far
enough beyond the pair that he felt safe in resuming his song.
He picked up where he left off, and continued his serenade
until he reached the bus stop at the end of the driveway.

As always, he had timed his walk to coincide precisely
with the expected arrival of the school bus that transported him
to work. For the bus to be on time, it had to arrive between
7:54:00 and 7:54:30. If it arrived 20 seconds too soon, the bus
driver received a reprimand for being early; exceeding the time
window brought an accusatory, "You're late!"

Unfortunately, his fellow passengers didn't share Jim's
respect for time. As a result, the bus driver and Jim's family
heard almost daily, in tones one might employ to accuse a vile
felon of unspeakable crimes against humanity, that the bus was
either Early or Late.

Once satisfied that the duly chastised driver wouldn't let it
happen again (at least until tomorrow), Jim boarded the bus
and seated himself for the short ride to school. His fellow
passengers were local teens, bound for high schools in the
neighboring towns of Ninilchik and Homer. Most of them spent
their elementary days at Chapman School, so were well-acquainted with Jim. Some greeted him as he sat down; he returned the greetings, all the while watching for signs of
overexuberance or rowdiness. Rules were rules; those kids had
better behave while Jim's eye was on them, or he'd have something to say about it.

The bus pulled up to the school, and Jim disembarked,
eyes already scanning for jobs that needed his attention. The
ground was dotted with puddles left by melting snow. Jim
welcomed the end of winter and the cessation of one of his
least favorite jobs: shoveling snow. Though normally respectful
of those in authority, he had engaged in several heated exchanges with the principal over the past months over exactly
whose responsibility it was to keep the walks clean. Jim favored
the job-sharing approach: "I did it last time; now it's your
turn." He felt the principal's statement, "It's your job–I have
other work to do," was simply a cop-out to avoid the hard
work.

This attitude toward snow shoveling might appear inconsistent, since in most instances Jim jealously guarded his claim

103

on as many jobs as possible. However, anyone who has moved an appreciable amount of snow by hand knows the physical strength and stamina demanded of the shoveler. Despite Jim's active life, he couldn't fully counteract the effects of Down's syndrome, which saddled him with low muscle tone. That predisposition made tasks which the rest of us find physically challenging, downright grueling for Jim, hence, he sought to avoid them.

Mrs. Henwood, a teacher and longtime ally of Jim's, sometimes intervened before the shoveling argument reached an impasse. Grabbing the shovel, she would say briskly, "Come on, Jim, I'll help you get that sidewalk cleared." Soothed by this show of support, Jim went willingly and stuck with the job till it was completed.

On this day, with spring in the air, sidewalk shoveling and its acrimonious discussions faded into hazy memory. A new task had emerged–literally out of the snow–in the form of trash. All sorts of garbage that spent the winter nestled under the snow or tossed about by the wind now sat in plain sight. His boss, the head custodian, directed him to the task. Hustling out with a trash bag, he made short work of the litter, all the while carrying on a lively self-discussion on the irresponsibility of those who throw trash on the ground in the first place.

Depositing the last soggy piece of paper into his trash bag, he eyed the yard. Satisfied with his efforts, he heaved the bag into the big dumpster, then moved inside the school to start his regular routine. His first stop was at the office to check in with the secretary.

"Hi, Marge."

"Hi, Jim," Marge replied, then watched as he disappeared toward the custodians' room to hang up his coat. She chuckled, remembering a recent morning when she thought they were the only two in the building. She had been surprised by the sound of voices coming from the custodians' room. She heard Jim's voice, then an unfamiliar man answering him. She really got spooked by the stranger's loud, evil-sounding laugh, "HA-HA-HO-HO-HO!"

Curious, she went to investigate. There sat Jim, all alone. "Jim!" she said, "Who were you talking to?"

"My other head," he replied. (Obviously, Marge wasn't acquainted with his buddies.)

"Well, after this, leave your 'other head' at home. You

scared me!"

Jim had laughed and promised, probably a little embarrassed that he'd been overheard.

Now, after hanging his coat neatly in its place, he poked
his head back into the office.

"Hey, Marge?"

Marge knew what was coming. This had become a special ritual
between the two of them. She didn't disappoint him: "Yes, Jim?"

"I lub you."

"I love you too, Jim."

Smiling, he continued his morning routine with a cruise down
the hall to unlock classroom doors and greet the early arrivals among
the staff. In addition to the standard "Good morning," the teachers
received a verbal list of all their students who recently transgressed a
rule. Jim had a great memory for rule-breakers and felt it was his duty
to report each one to the proper authority.

He had another mission on this trip to the classrooms:
passing out newspapers. A carrier dropped off the Anchorage
newspaper each morning, setting a pile of them in the staff
room, where the teachers could pick one up if they wanted it.
That wasn't good enough for Jim, so he had made it another of
his daily tasks to see that each classroom received the paper. He
couldn't read it, but he'd seen how much time his dad spent
perusing it, so he figured it must be important. The teachers,
whether or not they would have picked up a paper on their
own, appreciated Jim's solicitude in making this daily delivery.

The next job on his mental list was the water fountain.
Back when Uncle Bert trained him, he showed him how to
scrub the water fountain and told him that this would be his
job every morning. Bert had moved on, but the fountain remained. Jim gathered his cleaning supplies and went at the
task with zeal. Every move, from application of cleanser to the
scrubbing and rinsing, was performed just as he had been
shown by Bert.

At 8:15 Jim peered at his watch, knowing it was about time
for the buses to start rolling in. His expression relaxed as he
saw the first long yellow bus pull up and discharge its passengers. Jim greeted the students as they streamed through the
door, reminding them to wipe their feet; he knew how much
extra work was created by muddy shoes and boots. He loved
the early-morning activity and made sure his tasks kept him in

the vicinity of the office. Telephone calls often came in at this time of day; if he was on hand the secretary entrusted him with messages. Clutching each small yellow scrap, he hustled down to the appropriate room and delivered it to its intended recipient. The teachers also relied on him to take messages back to the office throughout the day.

Jim again consulted his watch. It was 8:40—time for school to start. Right on time, the bell rang. It was followed by a period of quiet as the classes began their day. This lull signaled to Jim that it was time to collect attendance slips. Down the hall he moved, stopping at each door to pick up the small slip of paper. Finished, he handed them over to Marge with all the care of a Loomis driver delivering a load of gold bullion.

Next, he prepared to put up the flags. Anyone stopping by the school early in the morning could view the special ritual Jim had created around his daily flag-raising. Pacing with stately tread, as if his entire entourage of buddies were parading behind him, he solemnly carried Old Glory and the Alaska flag out to the flagpole. There, he carefully fastened them in their appointed positions and raised them to the top of the pole. He then took a step back and smartly saluted the banners as they flapped in the breeze. (On days when he was feeling especially patriotic, occupants of the school heard a garbled but heartfelt rendition of "The Star Spangled Banner" wafting through the entryway and down the halls.)

He headed back inside for his daily check-in at one of his favorite classes, Donna Austin's kindergarten. He related to these youngsters' struggles with the alphabet and unraveling the mystery of numbers. This was the level of skill that he himself found challenging. Donna welcomed him in and encouraged children to show him their work. Jim scanned each paper with an appreciative eye, then, with a hug and an enthusiastic "Good job!" sent the proud student back to the group.

Throughout the morning, Jim kept busy with a variety of tasks. The food-service truck arrived, carrying milk and other supplies for lunch. Jim rushed out to assist the kitchen staff with the unloading. Busy teachers called on him for everything from carrying messages to moving desks, fetching supplies and cleaning up the occasional mess.

Shortly before lunchtime came one of the proudest tasks of Jim's work day: picking up the mail. He went to the office, where Marge handed him the letters and packages to be mailed, as well as money for postage. These he carefully placed in the canvas bag he hung around his neck by its handles. Then he walked the short distance along Anchor Point's main road from the school to the post office. Going to the window, he slipped the letters into the slot and handed packages and money to the postmistress. The change went back into the mail pouch. Jim knew the number of the school's mailbox, and used his post office key to open it. The mail joined the change in the pouch, and he returned to the window with several package notices. Carefully putting as much as possible into his pouch and firmly clutching the rest, the janitor-turned-mailman reversed his route and delivered the mail safely to Marge.

Marge learned the hard way that she shouldn't mess with Jim's routine. Once day she had occasion to make an early-morning trip to the local general store, which was attached to the post office. Thinking she'd save Jim a trip, she picked up the mail while she was there. When informed of this perfidy, Jim was incensed. In his mind, there was absolutely no good reason for her usurping his job. She apologized profusely, but it took several days before he recovered enough to completely forgive her.

The post office staff, also, occasionally felt Jim's wrath. There were days when, through no fault of anyone at the post office, the mail had not arrived by the time Jim made his daily visit. On these infrequent occasions, he sternly admonished the unfortunate postmistress, holding her personally responsible for avalanches, slick roads, snowstorms, or anything else that delayed the mail truck from Anchorage. He always was inclined to blame the messenger.

Just before noon came the time to set up the gym for lunch. Jim fetched the tables and benches from their storage room and wheeled them into position. He could feel the energy building as the kitchen crew readied the dishes for the onslaught of students. Smells swirled through the building, reminding Jim that, aside from a cup of coffee at break time, he hadn't eaten for hours.

Though many may cast aspersions upon school lunches, you would never hear any grumbling about it from Jim. The meal was a high point in his day, and he ate it with uncritical appreciation.

The kids were coming; Jim stationed himself just inside the lunchroom door where he could greet each student. The first class approached. He extended his hand. Students' and custodian's palms smacked together in a high-five, their favorite greeting. The children filed in, each receiving a welcoming hand from Jim. He continued to greet kids till he saw he was needed behind the counter. He took up his position, handing each child a carton of milk and the packet containing their utensils.

Gerry, the head cook, knew that, despite Jim's seeming concentration, his mind was working like an accountant's. He'd seen his friends in the kitchen adding up and calculating the number of trays and milk cartons that got used each day. He knew it was important, so he mentally stored up the numbers and stood ready any time within the next week, to report the day's statistics to anyone who wished to know.

After they picked up their meals and filtered over to the lunch tables, some students ate with a decorum and restraint admirable in youngsters surrounded by a multitude of friends. Others displayed a lunchtime etiquette that would embarrass a pack of ravenous hyenas. Jim couldn't know that this latter group, far from being an Anchor Point anomaly, shows up wherever school lunches are served.

Once the kids were served, Jim picked up his own lunch. He joked with the cooks as they filled his tray. They spoiled him dreadfully, giving him extra portions of his favorite things, slipping special treats to him on the sly. This brought no argument from Jim, who consumed everything on the tray and would eat more if given the opportunity.

He seated himself at one of the tables, trying to enjoy his lunch while witnessing rules being broken on a major scale. Occasionally he couldn't stand it, and jumped up to reprove this kid or scold that one, storing up names and faces in his memory, to be faithfully reported to the appropriate teachers at the first opportunity (and probably several more instances after that).

Some of the kids finished eating and took their trays to the trash can, where they dumped the remnants of their meal. When they started banging their trays unnecessarily hard, though, he knew he needed to call in reinforcements. In his mind, the rule "No banging trays" was inviolable. The trouble was, the kids didn't understand the importance of it. Quickly, he hustled down the hall in search of his friend, Mrs. Henwood.

"Mrs. Henwood, the kids are banging the trays," he intoned. Mrs. Henwood knew that nothing short of handcuffs would eliminate the tray banging entirely, but she recognized Jim's need for validation. Together they marched back to the lunchroom where, in her best no-nonsense teacher voice, she boomed, "Quit banging the trays!" A few students took heed, and the noise lessened infinitesimally. Temporarily satisfied, Jim finished his lunch, then embarked on trash patrol, darting in, snatching up food wrappers and milk cartons almost before they could reach the floor. The kids accepted him as a part of the school experience, unaware that a custodian like Jim was not a common sight.

A new kid—an eighth grader—was anxious to impress the cute, popular girl sitting across the table. Yelling and throwing food, he quickly attracted everyone's attention, Jim's included. "Hey, you kid!" (Jim didn't know his name yet.) "You simmer down there."

The youngster saw an easy target: "Yeah, are you gonna make me? You're just a re-tard!"

Jim knew he'd been insulted, and tried to respond, scolding the kid and repeating the rules of the lunchroom. His tormentor continued baiting him, laughing at his confusion, taunting him verbally, while openly flouting as many rules as he could. Finally, Jim realized he couldn't win this one and stalked angrily away. Though he was hurt, he found solace in the knowledge that he had important work to do. Throwing himself into his tasks, he pushed thoughts of the show-off to the back of his mind, comforting himself with the knowledge that the kid's teacher would be receiving a full report at the earliest possible moment.

Meanwhile, the new kid was receiving a lesson in manners from his fellow diners. Instead of responding, as he expected, with laughter and words of support, his peers appeared horrified. After a second or two of shocked silence, the cute girl rounded on him: "Don't you talk to him like that. That's Jim and he's our janitor and we love him, so you just leave him alone!"

The lunch period ended, and the kids headed out to recess. The head custodian made the rounds of the cafeteria with a large damp cloth, wiping off benches and tables. As soon

109

as they were cleaned, Jim wheeled them back to the storage room, their role completed for another day. With the furniture cleared away, the full effects of young and sloppy eaters were plain to see. Arming himself with a huge push broom, Jim gathered mounds of litter, scooped it into the dustpan, and deposited it in the trash can. He swept the floor thoroughly, clearing the way for the head custodian's mop, knowing that the room must soon be ready for its other life as a gymnasium.

Jim hurried to finish the floor. He kept one ear cocked for the sound of the bell which would ring soon, signaling the end of recess. He had made it his personal duty to monitor the children as they came back inside from the playground. Hearing the bell, he rushed to the hall and stood sentry, skewering with a look those intrepid enough to enter with undue speed or noise. Once the kids were safely and quietly back in their classes, he turned again to his other tasks.

As soon as the cooks had finished washing up the lunch mess, he knew it was time to mop the kitchen floor. Carefully he swabbed, concentrating on the job as if the future of our entire nation depended on its successful completion.

Throughout the afternoon, he kept busy, performing more of the same types of jobs he'd done in the morning. Between the secretary, principal, boss custodian and teachers, there was always something to do. No matter how busy he was, though, he managed to squeeze into almost every conversation the news that was foremost in his mind, "My birthday's comin'. May 9."

He knew these little seeds of information, when left to take root, would blossom into a fine party by the time the date arrived. It had become a tradition at the school. The eighth grade were in charge of the gift—usually a tee shirt, baseball cap, or mug bearing a special message. The cooks made a cake, and every class created handmade birthday cards. The entire student body gathered in the gym, then called Jim in. As everyone sang "Happy Birthday," he managed to act surprised, as if he hadn't shamelessly promoted this very event on a daily—indeed, hourly—basis for the last several months.

Almost before he knew it, his watch told him it was 3:00—time to say good-by to the kindergartners. He sent them off with a round of hugs and a chorus of "Good-bye, Jim!" then saw the older kids out the door and onto the buses.

As soon as they left, he grabbed the trash cart and began

his afternoon rounds. At each classroom, he gathered trash bags, piling them onto the cart. Some teachers had begun thinning out their stores of school supply catalogs, anticipating the end of the school year. Jim considered this a personal affront, as the catalogs weighed down the trash bags, making them almost too heavy to lift. He made sure he pointed out this failing to the transgressors, who took it in good spirit. They understood that he liked things a certain way, and change upset him. They apologized, he forgave them, and all was peaceful once more. He heaved the bags of trash, catalogs and all, into the big dumpster outside with the satisfaction of one to whom tidiness and order rank not too far behind godliness.

A few boys were shooting baskets in the gym. Seeing Jim, one of them called to him, "Hey Jim, wanna play?" With only one more task slated for the day, he felt he had time to briefly join them. They included him without giving it a second thought. Though they could play circles around him or ignore him entirely, they adapted their game. Jim caught rebounds, passed and received the ball, and even scored a couple of baskets. Finally, with their cheers ringing in his ears, he strutted off the court, confidence surrounding him like an aura.

His last job was another of his favorites: cleaning under the gym's bleachers. The attraction of such a job became apparent when a triumphant "Oh-ho!" emanated from the cramped space behind the stands. Jim's smiling face emerged, then his hand, tightly clutching a penny. He had discovered that, after a bleacher-sitting event, money often got left for him to find. That one penny made the whole dirty job worthwhile. The amount he found was not important, the finding itself tickled him.

Suddenly Jim's inner clock—which rarely failed him— warned him to check his watch once again. Sure enough, it was time to gather his things to go home. He took up a watchful position near the front door. Right on time, the high school bus pulled into the yard, signaling the end of his work day. He quickly ran back to the office. "Hey, Marge?"

"Yes, Jim."

"I lub you."

"I love you, too, Jim."

He strode confidently to the bus and climbed aboard, secure in the knowledge that he had done a good job and his school was better because of his efforts.

Church

The zeal that Jim had for God, from his youngest years, never faded; in fact, as he gained confidence in his school job, he grew determined to take a more active role in the church, as well. The Church of Christ in Anchor Point was a small, close-knit group. Several members worked with Jim at the school. Others had known him since we moved to Anchor Point and began attending the church in 1955. New arrivals didn't remain strangers to Jim for long, and could count on a weekly handshake, accompanied by a big smile and enthusiastic greeting.

Church dress codes in Alaska differ somewhat from those one often expects in the Lower 48. We see anything from snow-machine suits and bunny boots in winter to rain gear and fishing waders in summer. Jim, however, dressed with his usual care and forethought. On Saturday evening he polished and shined his dress shoes, and set out his "suit:" sport jacket, dress slacks with coordinating shirt, and clip-on tie (this is about as close to a suit as many Alaskans ever get). The fact that he and the preacher were usually the only ones wearing ties didn't faze him a bit. He liked dressing nicely, and used this avenue to show respect for the worship of his Lord.

When we were younger, if the rest of us had study books to complete before Bible class, we would be frantically working on them on Sunday morning before leaving for services. Jim prepared for class by getting his Bible (though he couldn't read) and a piece of paper (though his writing consisted of random letters). He would scrutinize a page in the Bible, with his nose almost touching the paper, then carefully print a string of letters, or his own scribble.

Sunday afternoons, or on days when he was not otherwise occupied, Jim held church services at home. A box set on top of a chair became a pulpit and all the other chairs in the house were lined up in rows to serve as pews for the congregation. He collected every Bible and song book he could lay his hands on, and arranged them on his pulpit. Then the service would begin, with Jim playing multiple roles as song leader, preacher, congregation, and even, at times, Devil's Advocate.

He usually began with a few songs, which he belted out with unselfconscious abandon. Had the writers of the words or the tunes been present, they would have been hard pressed to recognize their compositions, but Jim sang 'em as he heard 'em. It didn't matter whether or not we could understand them—he wasn't singing to us, anyway. Usually there was some snippet of his rendition that bore enough resemblance to the original that we could identify it, despite its variations. (Since we don't use instrumental accompaniment in worship, we're used to singing out strongly; those who can often choose to harmonize with an alto, tenor or bass line. Jim's selections reflected the bass or alto leads in some of these songs).

Our dad often served as song leader for our congregation, and would write a list of the songs he planned to lead on a scrap of paper. Many times I found long lists of song book numbers in Jim's handwriting lying around the house, and assumed that he was just imitating Dad's custom, without truly knowing what the numbers meant. One day Jim brought his list proudly to me and invited me to look at it. I don't know why, but I took the list and looked at the first number.

"What's number 220?" I asked.

" 'Onward, Crispy Shoulders,'" came the unhesitating reply. From long experience in translating Jim's particular brand of English, I knew he meant "Onward, Christian Soldiers." I looked it up: sure enough—that's what it was.

Well, anyone can be right once. I tried the next number: "What's 546?"

" 'Sneeze Go Home.'" Right again—the song was entitled, "The Way of the Cross," but Jim knew it by its first line, "I must needs go home."

In amazement, I read all of the thirty or so numbers on his list, and he reeled off the names of every song. I found that pretty impressive for someone who couldn't read more than a few sight words.

But getting back to his church service: after singing a few songs, he led a prayer. When Jim prayed, whether in these solitary services or saying grace before meals, he always said a heartfelt prayer, naming everyone he knew who was in need of a good word. He spoke his prayers at a much faster rate than his normal speech, so they were very difficult to understand—for us at least. I'm sure the Almighty took in every word just fine. We were able to catch only occasional phrases as he rattled on, but what we could pick up was touching, as he prayed for travelers, the sick, anyone he knew who was hurting in any way.

Once he had finished the prayer, he moved on to the sermon itself. He began by opening the Bible and "reading" a few "squishers" (his pronunciation of "scriptures"). His imaginary congregation must have been a noisy, mouthy bunch, because he often interrupted himself to snap his fingers and point at a certain chair with a stern look as if to say, "That is *not* the way to behave in church!" He then continued, only to interrupt himself again, this time with an argument. After a minute or so of heated exchanges, he thundered, "Look...Squishers say!" And that settled it. Though I never witnessed an argument during an actual church service such as he had going in his congregation, he had the gist of it right. Just as we accept the scriptures as the final authority, so did he.

We referred to Jim's boisterous services as "playing church," but he took his religion very seriously indeed. One summer when he was near thirty, a word we couldn't quite interpret began creeping into his sermons. Soon he was telling everyone, "I'm gonna be 'bat-tiss.'"

On a Sunday morning that summer I was sitting in the pew behind Mom and Jim, Dad being up front in order to lead singing. As the preacher wound down his sermon, he issued an invitation: "If you'd like to ask for the prayers of the church, or if anyone wants to have their sins washed away through baptism, please come forward as we stand and sing." Standing to sing an invitation song is our custom, meant to encourage those who want to respond but might feel a little shy.

As we all stood up, I noticed Jim trying to get out of the pew, but someone was standing in the way, singing, oblivious to Jim's efforts to leave. Suddenly his face contorted, and he started to weep. I poked Mom and motioned to Jim; she immediately started trying to find out what was wrong. She couldn't hear or understand him, as the congregation continued singing, so she took his arm and led him out of the auditorium. Dad soon joined them, thinking that Jim had gotten sick. In the back hallway, where it was quieter, he kept repeating, "I gotta be bat-tiss." They must have looked blank, because he suddenly put both hands to his chest and said plaintively, "I want Jesus in my heart!"

Aha! They finally realized that Jim wanted to be baptized. Although we believe that the Bible teaches immersion in water as a necessary step in God's plan of salvation, it hadn't occurred to my parents that Jim needed baptism, since in their eyes he was as innocent as a child. He obviously looked at it differently, feeling that he wanted to be right with his God in every possible way.

Well, who were we to stand in the way of a penitent believer? The congregation piled out of the church building to witness Jim's baptism. We didn't have a baptistery at this point, so the group headed to where there was, in Biblical terms, "much water:" the icy-cold currents of the North Fork River.

As we gathered on the banks of the stream, I thought back to my baptism, also in the North Fork. Being an Alaska kid who had never seen a body of water that looked warm enough in which to submerge my person, I had never before that day had my head completely underwater. Now I wondered how Jim, with no more aquatic experience than I, was going to take to this immersion in forty-some-degree water.

He walked confidently out to the wader-clad preacher, who awaited him in the deepest part of the stream. His stride checked only slightly as the chilly current swirled first around his legs, then crept up almost to his waist. The preacher briefly explained the symbolism of baptism, how it parallels the death, burial, and resurrection of Christ. Then he got a good grip on Jim, showed him how to put his hand over his nose and mouth, and dunked him.

Jim shot up out of the water like a breaching whale; hands and feet flinging water and rocks in all directions as he scrambled toward shore, looking rather wild of eye and blue around the gills. We come prepared to these gatherings, though, and soon had him cocooned in warm blankets, getting hugs and handshakes from everyone. Once the shock of the cold wore off, the smile on his face told us all that his limited vocabulary could not. He had obeyed the Lord's command and was at peace in his soul.

As in all aspects of his life, Jim looked constantly for opportunities to take on new tasks at church. After watching one of the men leave the adults' Bible class each Sunday to knock on the doors of the children's classrooms, Jim campaigned for the job. It was a perfect fit: he loved doing things by the clock, and there was a specified time to knock on those doors. If he was supposed to knock at 10:50 he would begin peering at his watch about 10:30. Every few minutes he checked again, turning to compare his watch time to the clock in the back of the auditorium. At 10:50—on the dot—he popped up and headed down the stairs to knock the doors. And woe betide any unsuspecting soul who might leave the auditorium within 5 minutes of Jim's appointed time, even for such a benign purpose as a trip to the bathroom. Obviously believing that the only reason to be moving about was to usurp his job, Jim leapt up and overtook the person by the time he or she reached the back of the auditorium. He then took up a watchful stance—timepiece in hand—at the top of the stairs until the appointed minute arrived.

Another job he performed on a regular basis was helping to serve communion. Usually several people are asked to help; they move from pew to pew, passing the communion plates around to the members. Jim observed the weekly routine over the course of several years, then approached Don, the man in charge of organizing the helpers and urged him to let him lend a hand. Don checked with Dad, who was pleased that Jim wanted to help, then allowed Jim to assist. He performed the task flawlessly and proudly, and continued to do so for many years.

There was also the matter of lights and heat. After every service he made the rounds of the auditorium, lowering the setting on the thermostats and turning off any light that appeared to be unused. I'm sure he saved the church hundreds of dollars over the years by his vigilance.

During special presentations involving a slide show or a movie, Jim would trip over chairs, his feet, and/or other people to be the first one to the light switch. He then hovered there, ensuring that he got to turn the lights back on.

All these chores were simple, but when Jim saw that he was able to do them, he went after them and made them his own. Many of us have the ability to do much more, yet we leave our talents untapped, focusing instead on what we can't do, rather than finding out where our strengths lie. Jim wasn't able to read the Bible that he carried so faithfully to church, yet he lived as if he had read and committed to memory Colossians 3:23: "Whatever you do, work at it with all your heart, as working for the Lord, not for men." Just as he performed his tasks at school and home to the very best of his ability, so he did at church. In spite of his limitations, he gave all he had, willingly, with all his heart, and considered himself privileged to serve.

The Big One

Jim never became a fan of commercial fishing, but he did enjoy going out with Dad for a day of sport fishing. Especially for halibut.

A halibut is a one of God's odder-looking creatures. It can range in size from a few pounds to several hundred. It swims with its flat belly-side down along the sandy bottom of the ocean, so that a large one looks rather like a piece of plywood with fins. The eyes, as one would imagine, are on the upper side of its body. Common sense would suggest that the mouth would then be on the underside. Alas, common sense would be mistaken. Consider instead that someone has taken a saw and cut a gash in the end of our piece of plywood at ninety degrees to the position of the eyes. Now you have a more accurate picture of the humble, homely halibut.

When pulled from the dingy depths in which it lives, a more unlovely creature would be difficult to imagine. Nevertheless, the halibut is pursued by commercial and sport fishermen alike for the tender, succulent flesh hidden under its ugly—not to mention smelly—exterior.

By the mid-1980s, Dad had semiretired from active fishing, and passed the boat on to my brother Ron and his family. He still felt the call of the sea, though, so occasionally he and Jim would take a skiff down to the beach off of Anchor Point and go out for a day of halibut sport fishing.

On one sunny, calm day they went out for a few hours of easy fishing. Unfortunately, either the halibut weren't interested in the bait they were offering or they were fishing in the wrong place. To make matters worse, the wind picked up. Previous experience had taught Jim that a boat was not the best place to be in rough weather—even with Dad along—so Dad soon headed back toward shore.

There is no dock on the Anchor Point beach, so the accepted method of getting ashore is to wait for a good wave and run the boat up a short distance onto the beach. This takes some coordination: the driver has to pull the outboard motor up at the proper moment so it doesn't run into the sand. Then the operator, or his companion, must leap nimbly from the boat and, on the next wave, pull the boat as far as possible onto the shore. Nimble leaping was not high up in Jim's repertoire of skills, so Dad ran the boat up, leapt out, and prepared to pull it ashore.

He miscalculated slightly, though, and a mischievous wave caught the boat, causing it to turn broadside and flip over. Its hapless passenger was deposited unceremoniously into the icy surf, trapped under the boat. Fortunately, they were in shallow water, so Jim was more scared than threatened with any real danger. The next wave washed enough water under the boat for Dad to get his hands under the gunwale. With a mighty shove he lifted the side up, allowing Jim to scramble out. He lunged from the water, gasping in what may have been the understatement of his life, "I'm wet! It's cold!"

A mere dunking in frigid water failed to quench the taste for halibut, so another pretty day found Dad and Jim again setting out, filled with the eternal hope that springs within every real fisherman. This particular day—fortunately, considering succeeding events—Dad opted to run out only a few hundred yards off the beach, and they dropped their lines in about 15 feet of water.

After several hours of fishing with no noticeable product to show for it, Dad decided that he'd had enough. He told Jim, "We might as well quit...reel in your line and let's go home." He cranked in his own gear and went to pull the anchor.

Jim, valiantly pulling on his pole, said, "I can't get mine up." Dad went over to see if perhaps he'd gotten his line caught on a rock or something, when suddenly the "something" took off. Jim's reel screamed as line whizzed off and disappeared beneath the water's surface. Together, he and Dad wrestled the writhing pole, managing to slow and finally stop the line's escape.

Inch by inch, they reeled the line back in, forcing the reluctant halibut on the other end to return from wherever he was headed. All the while, Dad was wondering, "Now what?" He didn't know how big the fish was, but from its antics it had to be more than a "chicken," the term applied to the small, five- to ten-pound types. When they finally got it to the surface, Dad knew immediately that pulling it aboard was not an option. It was big enough and feisty enough to do real damage to them and the boat.

Dad was doubly glad he'd decided against running out that day to distant halibut grounds. At least they only had a short hop to shore. Deciding to tow it in, he showed Jim how to hold the pole to keep it steady, while he idled the boat slowly in to shore.

Jim's catch was not a monster by halibut standards, being only 70 pounds, but it was a trophy to him. His first words to me upon arriving home were, "Get your camera; take a picture." The Big One that didn't get away remained one of his favorite memories throughout his life.

Jimisms

Most families have sayings that originated when their children were learning to talk and/or discovering the ways of the world. Children have a fresh, innocent take on things that often sticks with us because they are able to see mundane events in a new light. I feel we were especially privileged in this regard, since Jim retained that childlike view of the world throughout his life. We ended up with a wealth of "Jimisms" thanks to Jim's long and voluble life.

As kids, when one of us got into trouble over a misdeed that Mom or Dad had discovered through unknown means, the unlucky one would naturally grill the siblings to see who had tattled. Jim's response was emphatic: "I not say nuthin'!" He refused to take the blame for something he didn't do. Even as an adult, there were times when a conversation between several family members might grow a little heated. Jim may not follow the gist of it, but he had the uneasy feeling that someone was about to get blamed for something. If anyone's gaze happened to rest on him during one of these exchanges, his claim again came quickly and with feeling, "I not say nuthin'!" We still find it a useful phrase when tempers get a little hot and need to be cooled with a touch of humor.

Jim loved to socialize, especially if there was food involved. During holidays, when there were many relatives around, meals—especially breakfasts—were eaten in shifts that went on for hours. Since Jim was an early riser, he ate with the early crew. When the next group appeared, Jim would again seat himself at the table, enjoying the conversation and congenial atmosphere. Soon the food would become an overwhelming temptation. As he reached for a morsel, he'd casually comment, "I'm-a say *dat* one" as his cover-up phrase. (It probably came from hearing others say something like, "You can say *that* again.") We soon learned that Jim's saying that was a signal that he was sneaking an extra meal. I've heard my other brothers use it many times when they knew they were eating beyond their own reasonable limits.

He had the solution to his overeating, though. When anyone called him on it, he'd say, "I'm gonna cut down tomorrow." How often have we all heard that! The problem for Jim was, he didn't realize tomorrow, truly, never comes. Thanks to his activity level and Mom's vigilance, he kept his weight within a healthy range, but it could easily have been otherwise.

Since most folks did not think to consult Jim before naming their children, his inexpert oral motor apparatus did the best it could to pronounce the results of baby-naming run wild. Even some of his brothers, whom one would think would have known better, married women whose names were difficult for Jim to wrap his tongue around. Tim's wife Melody became Mud-o-dee, and John's Celeste' was Lesky.

Others' names which he could pronounce he sometimes changed for reasons known only to him. Shortly after a new principal took over at the school, the name "Freddy" began to feature prominently in Jim's tales from work. Dad discovered that, sure enough, the principal's name was Fred: he tried to explain that calling the principal Freddy might be interpreted as disrespectful. That cut no ice with Jim; he called the guy Freddy, and Freddy he would remain. When Dad finally got a chance to talk to Fred, he tried to apologize in case Jim had caused offense. Fred laughed, saying, "Nobody's ever called me Freddy except for my parents. I don't mind—it makes me feel like I'm really at home."

Jim's language difficulties did not slow him down or discourage him from talking. He heard and spoke words differently than we did, but he usually got his point across. When he had trouble making us understand, he walked us through it with patience and good humor. Throughout his years of working at the school, Jim and Dad had a nightly ritual in which Jim would report on what the school served that day for hot lunch. Sometimes, when the entree was a dish that wasn't common on our dinner table, the conversation got rather bewildering.

Dad: "What did you have for lunch today?"

Jim: "Widows."

"What?!"

"Widows." This time he spoke, helpfully, slightly louder, in case Dad was having trouble hearing.

"*Widows?*"

"No, *widows.*"

A guessing game ensued, with us trying to figure out what he'd eaten. At each incorrect guess, Jim would throw back his head and guffaw. If we failed to come up with the correct answer, we eventually had to quit as we ran out of guesses. At this, Jim would venture a further explanation to clarify: "Widows...dey got da bean in 'em."

"Oh! Burritos?"

"Yeah—widows."

Jim's role as benevolent dictator of Chapman School regarding all behaviors acceptable and proper was one not easily relinquished, either by him or his subjects. It was not difficult to spot children who attended "his" school; if Jim reproved them—regardless of the setting, they generally responded immediately.

I recall a birthday party, after Jim had retired, that showed he still wielded a great deal of authority. Whenever any of us who lived in the vicinity of my parents had a birthday, Mom made a cake. She didn't have to invite anyone or advise us that the cake was there; toward evening, as if drawn by some unseen force, a group began to gather at my parents' house, including some relatives we may not have seen since the last birthday. (And of course, there was still the toothpick factor. The ones she inserted in later years had dropped their colored coats and appeared *au naturel*, but their worth had increased to a buck a piece, so everyone still searched avidly for them.)

At one of these impromptu parties, a young nephew of mine showed up with a new girlfriend. Whether due to a shortage of chairs, uneasiness in a group she didn't know well, or just because she wanted to, the young lady chose to sit on my nephew's knee. Our family does not make a habit of sitting on laps after the age of about four, but aside from a few amused glances no one took much notice of the couple. That is, until Jim came into the room and beheld the spectacle. In a tone of mingled indignation and laughter he exclaimed, "Get OFF his lap!"

Though it had been half a dozen years since she had heard Jim's voice ringing through the halls of elementary school, that girl popped off my nephew's lap as if someone had pushed an eject button. There was no doubt: when Jim spoke, she knew she'd better obey.

He had a unique view of such things as life, death and TV shows. He hated unhappy endings, and would watch a chosen movie whenever it appeared on television, apparently hoping that those responsible would finally get it right. "Davy Crockett" was a prime example. Each time, as Davy and his brave cohorts gamely fought the losing battle at the Alamo, Jim perched on the edge his chair, screaming at the television, "Look out! He's behind ya!" When it was all over, he'd stomp out of the room mumbling, "They'll get 'em next time."

He was an avid fan of "The Price is Right" and watched it any time it didn't conflict with his work schedule. He knew, not just Bob Barker, but all the folks who had a part in the show. One of these was Johnny Olsen, the man who announced the prizes and pumped up the crowd with his enthusiastic delivery. To Jim, Johnny Olsen was an irreplaceable part of the experience.

Well, sadly, Johnny Olsen went the way of all flesh, and a new announcer replaced him. This did not set well with Jim. If someone had a job to do, they needed to do it, and not let a little thing like death interfere with the completion of that task. He fretted and pouted; Mom explained that Johnny Olsen had died, and wouldn't be on the show anymore. It took several months, but finally Jim seemed to accept the fact that Johnny Olsen was really gone.

Then came the season of reruns. Guess who was back on "The Price is Right". Jim came beaming into the kitchen to tell Mom, "Johnny Olsen's back."

Mom, understandably taken aback, reminded him, "But he died, Jim."

With a look of utter astonishment he stared at her a moment, then asked unbelievingly, "*Again?!*"

Responsibility

Jim was never one to let his weak points get him down. Though he had the merest nodding acquaintance with traditional school subjects, he made up for those deficits by doing what he could do to the very best of his ability. His sense of responsibility, originally fostered during those early days with simple chores like the pajama lessons, bloomed and flourished in every aspect of his life. Part of this, I believe, stemmed from his conviction that the church, the school, and, indeed, our home would crumble to ruins if he weren't there to oversee operations.

Unlike many folks with Down's syndrome who suffer with heart and other major medical problems, Jim was blessed with good health. Aside from a bout with pneumonia as a child, he had few major illnesses through most of his life. Sometimes he'd complain about a pain, but one suggestion that maybe he should stay home and get well and miss either work or church, and he experienced a most miraculous cure. "I feel better now," he'd assure us. In one of his early years of work he came down with trench mouth. He ran a high fever, and was miserable from the sores in his mouth; still, Mom had to almost physically restrain him to keep him from heading out the door to fulfill his appointed jobs.

During the 1980s, my parents began taking a yearly road trip Outside to visit friends and relatives. Because the commercial fishing season lasted into August, they couldn't go until mid-August or later. They were generally gone for between three and four weeks; the original plan was to take Jim along and let him start work late, but he wouldn't hear of it. If his job started on August 10, he was going to be there August 10. Who cared about a vacation; there was work to be done!

The first time this happened, a quandary loomed for Mom and Dad. They had been Outside only three times in nearly thirty years; were they never to have another vacation because Jim had a job? The only solution to this dilemma seemed to be for Jim to stay at home on his own. Several of us siblings lived nearby and agreed to keep an eye on him.

The arrangement worked even better than my parents had hoped. Before the trip, Mom stocked the pantry with canned goods ranging from all-in-one-can dinners to fruit. (Having lived his life in rural Alaska, one thing Jim knew how to do was wield a can opener.)

While they were gone, his routine varied little. When his alarm sounded, he got up, showered and dressed, slipping into a short-sleeved polo shirt and double knit slacks. Breakfast consisted of coffee, and one of three options which he prepared competently: Rice Krispies with milk, oatmeal without milk, or eggs and toast. He usually topped this meal off with a banana, then washed his dishes. At 7:48—no sooner, no later—he headed out the driveway to meet the bus. He spent his day doing his job with the single-mindedness of someone who believed that his role was the critical hinge upon which all others' jobs depended.

After work, the bus dropped him at the end of the driveway, from whence he carefully looked both ways, then nipped across the road and collected the newspaper from its box. At home, he stacked the paper with all the others, then took the family mail (picked up on his daily school mail run) from his mailbag and sorted it by name: L for Lionel, E for Esther, and J for himself.

For supper he opened and heated a can of stew, chicken-and-noodles, or soup. Bread and butter, and cottage cheese with canned fruit usually accompanied this repast. Afterwards he washed his dishes—including the cans that his food came in—and decided what to have the next evening. When I dropped by in the evening to see how he was doing, I'd know immediately what he planned for tomorrow's main dish: the can already reposed on the kitchen counter with the can opener balancing neatly atop.

His evening entertainments included listening to the radio for all the important stuff—baseball games, weather, and the Dow Jones report; and watching TV for football games, "Jeopardy" and "Wheel of Fortune". When those avenues were exhausted, he kept busy conducting his own church services and the occasional parade on the driveway.

As bedtime neared, he put out his breakfast place setting with a bowl or plate, depending on what he intended to make for breakfast the next morning. After setting and resetting his watch to perfect sync with the kitchen clock, he headed upstairs to bed. There, the radio-alarm clock took its nightly abuse as Jim fiddled with the knobs, making sure the time was exactly set to the time on his watch.

On weekends, he and I went out for breakfast, and I also picked him up for church services. He let me know when his supply of milk, bread or other perishables was running low, and we went shopping.

Although he did not have the cognitive ability to live entirely independently—taking care of bills, repairs, or emergencies that might arise—he did very well during those short times on his own. He could even take some variations in his routine in stride. One evening while he was staying alone, we had a power outage. I decided to walk over and make sure he was not upset. I needn't have worried. As I approached the house, a dim light shone through the living room window. That was odd, I thought, with the power being out. I hoped Jim hadn't taken to lighting candles. Then I heard the voice of an announcer, giving a play-by-play of a baseball game.

Opening the door, I beheld a cozy scene: Jim had dug out the battery-operated lantern and transistor radio that Dad kept for just such contingencies. He had light and he had his ball game: obviously he didn't need any reassurance from me.

Of course, a phone call from Dad to update Jim on their travels eclipsed all other evening activities. A typical call might sound like this:

"Hello."

"Hi, Jim."

"Who's this?" (He always asked, even when he initiated the call.)

"It's me." (Dad feels he shouldn't ever have to identify himself by name when talking with a family member.)

"That you, Pa?"

"Yep, how're things going?"

"Oh, pretty good. Where you?"

"We just got to North Dakota today."

"What time you get there?"

"About 3 o'clock."

"What time you left?" (Where they left *from* didn't matter, just the time.)

"About 8 this morning."

"Hmmm—makin' good time."

For himself, Jim didn't enjoy traveling much. I think his comment, "Makin' good time" had more to do with the fact that the travelers were one day closer to their final destination—in other words, home—than it did his appreciation of the distance traveled. He always made the same comment, even if the vehicle in question had limped to the nearest roadhouse with a flat tire and busted radiator. Whatever his reasons were for making the statement, it has become one of our "Jim phrases" that we use in joking, but affectionate, remembrance whenever any of the family travels.

Special Days

"The outlook today calls for snow, continuing through tonight, with a possibility of flurries tomorrow." The radio announcer's voice was cheerful as he gave the forecast.

Jim's face reflected the gloominess of the skies outside. "I don't want snow! Pa, call the radio and tell 'em." He held weather forecasters personally responsible for any inclement weather.

As upset as he got over rain or snow, he was equally appreciative of nice weather. Any time the sun shone, he'd comment, "Pretty day." On warm summer days he took long walks along the mud path that paralleled the road. Well-meaning neighbors often stopped by the house to report seeing him, thinking he might be lost. My parents assured them that he was fine—he just wanted to savor the "pretty day."

Our part of Alaska is better known for clouds and drizzle than for sun, but one summer we received even more than our usual quota of rain and gray, overcast days. For every pretty day, a week went by when the sun never put in an appearance.

After experiencing this pattern for a month or so, Jim came to me one day, all excited. "Hey Mary, look—blue clouds." He pointed upward. Sure enough, I espied a small patch of blue sky where the sun struggled valiantly to chase away the clouds. I think the gray clouds won out over the blue clouds that day, but Jim kept looking, watching and hoping for clearing skies and more pretty days.

As much as pretty days, Jim loved special days. Birthdays—especially his own—were talked of for weeks and sometimes months in advance. He loved taking the birthday person out for dinner, and proudly produced his wallet to pay at the appropriate time. He trustingly handed the wallet over to one of us, and we dug out the correct total.

Going out to eat was a highlight in Jim's life. During our growing-up years, the cost of eating out with a family of nine was prohibitively expensive, so we rarely saw the inside of a restaurant. When our numbers eventually dwindled to a few, eating out became much more affordable. Sunday afternoons seemed the logical time for such an indulgence, since we were already in the car, and all dressed up.

Each week Dad began the ritual:

"Well, what should we do for lunch?"

Jim's reply came readily, if ambiguously, "It's up to you."

"I guess we'll just go home." Dad delighted in gently teasing him.

"I brought my wallet," Jim then offered. He always was one who thought ahead.

Sometimes I suspected that Jim's favorite part of going out to eat was the opportunity it afforded to socialize. As we walked into the local restaurant, a chorus of "Hi, Jim!" rose up from nearly every table. Jim worked the room, shaking hands and chatting with the assembled diners. The rest of us trailed along in his wake, receiving very little attention, except an occasional comment such as, "Oh, you're Jim's sister/mom/dad?"

One year, when May was barely peeping over April's shoulder, he approached Dad and queried, "Pa, what's your schedule for June 9?"

As June 9 was far away and had no special significance to my dad, he replied, "I really don't have a schedule. What's happening on June 9?"

" 'Fore I get off work." (Meaning, that was his last day of work before the custodians finished for the summer.) Starting his summer break was enough reason to celebrate, even though on the first day of vacation he began talking nonstop about going back to work in the fall. That day, too, would rate a celebratory dinner.

Taking family members out on their birthdays, anniversaries, or other special days was Jim's solution to the problem of presents. A meal at a restaurant remedied the situation nicely.

One year, on my brother Ken's birthday, Jim was looking forward to taking Ken, his wife, and their small children out to eat. Mom explained that might not be a good idea, because Ken's kids had food allergies that severely restricted their diets. She suggested that maybe he could think of something else to do for Ken.

"Then I'll just buy him a car," Jim decided. Fortunately, my parents had a better grasp on money matters than to allow that to happen!

Saturdays were special to Jim and me. We had a standing breakfast date for Saturday morning at Anchor Point's main restaurant, the Anchor River Inn. For about ten years, I could expect a Friday evening phone call from Jim, asking me if I planned to go to breakfast. (I suspect that he made the call not because he felt the need to confirm our date, but because he loved to use the phone.)

Me: Hello?
Jim: Who's this?
Me: Who did you call?
Jim: You.
Me: Then it's me.
Jim: You goin' to breakfast in the mornin'?
Me: Yep, you wanna go?
Jim: What time you goin'?
Me: 7:30.
Jim: Okay, bye.

On Saturday morning I picked him up at 7:30 (it's a good thing we were both morning people), and drove to the Inn. There, Jim ordered one of his three favorite choices: biscuits and gravy (half order), pancake combo (with scrambled eggs), or a mushroom omelet (no cheese). We chatted about his week at school, recent visitors to the house, or the latest winner on Jeopardy. And I could be sure, if the sun was at all in evidence, that before we left he'd throw in his standard comment, "Pretty day."

Every holiday from Memorial Day to Labor Day required a commemorative "click-nic" (Jim's word for picnic). Whatever the weather, around noon a circle of stones appeared in the yard, and a small mountain of sticks and branches grew beside it. Jim let us know, without a word, that it was a holiday and the hot dog fire was ready to burn. Many of these celebrations saw us swathed in parkas or raincoats, or stacking rocks on everything to keep our "click-nic" from blowing away, but despite the threat of imminent hypothermia, the day received its due.

Jim's Rig

May 9, 1979: Jim's thirty-fourth birthday. Dad got off work, and hurried to pick up Jim's present. He knew what he wanted to get–he just didn't know if he could make it to the store before they closed.

Dashing into the Soldotna Honda dealers, he was told they were about to close, but they'd stick around long enough to sell him a three-wheeler. The transaction completed, Dad loaded the shiny red machine into the back of his pickup. The salesman had one more bit of information: the big tires had such low air pressure that it wouldn't register with a pressure gauge, so to make sure they had equal pressure, he recommended measuring the circumference of the two back tires. If they were of unequal size, he instructed Dad to inflate the smaller tire until they measured the same.

The hour-long drive home seemed to drag by as he anticipated Jim's reaction. The look on Jim's face when he saw his present was priceless. He had wheels! Mom and Dad also gave him a helmet, which they stressed he must wear at all times when driving. Jim was fine with that—just let him at this three-wheeler, which he immediately began referring to as "my rig."

He mounted the vehicle, and Dad showed him how to start it. Putting it in first gear, he proceeded to drive—in circles. The salesman was right: the circumference of the tires did indeed need to be equal. Once that glitch was remedied, Jim was off down the driveway, and on to adventures he alone could create.

Jim's rig became much more than transportation, although that was one of its functions. His morning walk to the bus was replaced by a short drive. At the end of the driveway, he selected a sheltered spot beneath the trees, out of sight of anyone driving along the road. Here he parked his rig, set his helmet atop the seat, and carefully spread plastic over the whole (he never knew when it might rain, and he didn't want to drive home with a wet rear end.)

At day's end, the vehicle metamorphosed into anything Jim desired, from a police car with sirens wailing, to an updated version of his trusty steed Silver. (Thankfully, he resisted the temptation to leap off his rig as he had the old bicycle, but he managed to catch the bad guys just as well as ever.)

130

After a while, the quarter-mile long driveway became old hat, and Jim's eyes looked to expanding horizons. Like anyone with recently acquired driving skills and a new set of wheels, he desired to show off just a little.

The North Fork Road that runs past our driveway has evolved considerably since my father and brothers made that first grueling pass down its unwelcoming length. It now contains two relatively roomy paved lanes, flanked on either edge by narrow, semi-paved shoulders.

A large number of residents own all-terrain vehicles (ATVs) similar to Jim's rig, which, by law, are banned from driving the public roads. Over the years, a bumpy path of hard-packed mud has emerged, paralleling the North Fork Road. Its builders, for the most part, were the younger members of the community, who wanted to run their three- and four-wheelers, dirt bikes, and (in winter) snow machines as near as possible to the main road without running afoul of the law. In addition to ATVs, the path also now serves bikers, joggers, walkers, and even the occasional sled dog team — in short, anyone who is constrained, either by law or by choice, to avoid the dangers of the roadway.

As I said, the path's original users were mostly youngsters, anxious to see what power their rigs were capable of. Without helmets or any other form of protective gear, the kids sailed over bumps at whatever the top speed was of their particular vehicle, seemingly always attempting to get a little more air on each bump that they did on the last. A huge cloud of dust is a common sight on the path; upon closer inspection one will generally find a large ATV, a small person, and an even smaller amount of good judgment all rolling along together at the front of said cloud.

Jim's adventures with his rig often took him to the end of the driveway, from whence he could watch the antics of his fellow ATVers on their custom-made path. What they were doing looked like a lot of fun, so he reckoned he'd give it a try.

Here he reckoned without the vigilance of his parents. Other folks may drive the bumpy path at recklessly high rates of speed, apparently oblivious to the dangers of tearing around with nothing but one's fingertips in contact with the vehicle. It only took one report that someone had seen Jim driving down the path along the road-way–though with helmet donned and pace sedate–and Jim received an ultimatum: stay on the driveway, or lose the rig.

That was all it took. The driveway soon sported an extra pair of ruts in testament to the number of trips made, but he never again tried to drive farther than the end of the driveway. He wasn't about to lose his rig!

A few years later, when the dangers of three-wheelers became widely known, Jim upgraded to a four-wheeler, which he loved and operated with the same fervor and imagination he had lavished on the first vehicle.

Special Olympics

Though Jim loved all kinds of sports, he had never had an opportunity to play in games that were more organized than the softball games my brothers played on the back forty. That all changed one year, with his introduction to Special Olympics.

The first contact came through my job working with children with disabilities, and I brought the information to my parents. The mothers of two of my students, with assistance from me and a couple of other volunteers, spearheaded the beginnings of Special Olympics in Homer. We decided to make bowling our first Olympic event, partly because we thought it was something the kids would enjoy and be successful at, and partly because we had ready access to a bowling alley.

Jim, at the age of 42, was one of two adults to participate in that original group of twelve Olympians, with the majority of the participants under the age of ten. Only one of the entire group had ever held a bowling ball before. As a "coach" I felt almost as ignorant, since my prior visits to bowling alleys numbered exactly two.

Every Saturday morning we would gather to practice; Mark, the facility's big-hearted owner, allowed us to use the alleys and equipment for free. Those first weeks seemed to be spent more on teaching the coaches enough so that we could then teach the Olympians, but everyone slowly gained proficiency.

In typical fashion, Jim threw his heart into the game. Not for him the wandering around and socializing that some of the others indulged in. He kept track of whose turn was coming for his lane, and got disgusted when some weren't ready as quickly as he thought they should be. He occasionally employed his school voice to boss the younger kids around when he felt they needed it.

He loved the game, and loved the high-fives when he got a spare or a strike. Being zealous and dedicated did not necessarily mean that he was a great bowler; in fact, he was a very inconsistent scorer. His usual pattern was a relatively high score on the first game, thirty to forty points less on the second, then somewhere in between on the third.

My parents—who had never bowled in their lives—

brought Jim to practice each week, and recognized the benefits he was receiving from the activity and interaction with the other participants. Besides which, it just looked like a whole lot of fun. Before long, the three of them joined a league whose noncompetitive view of the game gave them a perfect way to learn and improve. All through the next several long, dark winters, they made the trip to Homer every Friday night to participate with their league.

Though Jim loved bowling for its own sake, the Special Olympics tournaments were an extra thrill for him. Our local games were held at the bowling alley; this gave a feeling of familiarity, yet there was the added excitement of having an audience and special activities. After the competition, Homer's mayor would give a short speech, then award medals and ribbons to the contestants. In Special Olympics, everyone who participates gets a medal or a ribbon, so everyone feels like a winner. The emphasis is not on *being* the best, but doing one's best. Though Jim saved and displayed his medals and ribbons proudly, his favorite ritual was marching in the procession.

As a finale, we always had a parade with Olympians carrying an American flag and the Olympic torch (a flashlight decked out with yellow and orange crepe paper making a dandy substitute for the real thing). During one tournament, Jim was chosen as flag-bearer, meaning he got to be the lead man. With a tape player blaring out one of his favorite Sousa marches, he solemnly marched in, shoulders back, eyes looking straight ahead, hands firm and proud as he held the flag high. As I watched, I thought of his parades up the driveway: here his rather lonely fantasy became a real, live event, complete with fellow-marchers, a cheering audience and music from some source other than his own throat.

From bowling, our local Special Olympics chapter branched out to include the events of swimming and skiing, but none ever resonated with Jim the way bowling did. As lifelong Alaskans, our opportunities to swim had been limited, and it showed. Jim loved the water, but made a better anchor than buoy. With access to the pool at the high school a mere one time per week, our emphasis was on making sure nobody drowned. Some of the younger kids demonstrated the benefits they had obtained from their years of schooling where they received swimming instruction. Jim, having missed out on that, was in it for the fun. And that was okay. He was in the thick of things, he was giving it his best effort, and he was enjoying himself.

We tried skiing for only one winter season. One might expect all Alaskans to be familiar with cross-country skiing, but that is not the case. Our family always had skates, but never skis. So Jim was over 40 before he first strapped on a pair of skis. During practice he shuffled along, never getting the hang of the gliding motion that separates the skiers from the shamblers. At our local competition, he was paired with the one male nearest his own age: a high school student who had been skiing for years. The boy had disabilities, but he knew how to ski. He flew by Jim and made several laps around the course before Jim was well-started. When Jim realized his poky pace was making him lose, he tried to hustle his shuffle. This of course threw him off balance, and down he went. Having never gone fast enough to fall before, this was a new experience for him: one that he didn't care to repeat. He somehow slogged his way to the finish line and got his second-place ribbon. When Mom expressed concern that falling was probably not good for his forty-some-year-old bones, she got no argument from Jim.

A year or so later, Homer Special Olympics was temporarily disbanded. This brought an end to Jim's participation in organized sports, though he continued to bowl when he could. Any time he and my parents got near a bowling alley, the three of them took the opportunity to throw a few games. In addition, the church sponsored some bowling parties, and, for Dad's eightieth birthday, we had a family bowling day, with about 30 family members present. Jim never got the highest score at any of these functions, but I doubt that anyone enjoyed them more than he did.

When I asked Jim what he wanted for his fiftieth birthday, he replied, "A trophy." Closer questioning elicited the information that he wanted a trophy like the ones he'd seen at the bowling alley. I approached Mark, our friend at the bowling alley, who supplied an old trophy from some long-forgotten contest. It had a figure of a man about to toss a bowling ball, and a plaque containing someone's name. My husband and I fashioned a new plaque, with Jim's name and a big 50 on it. Jim was delighted with it and displayed it as proudly and prominently as if he had actually won it in a bowling contest.

Beginning of Decline

At one of our Saturday breakfast dates I noticed the first signs that Jim was losing some of his abilities. Mom had mentioned that his speech was less clear, but I had not noticed, since I did not see him as often as she did. What I first noticed was the failing of some fine motor skills. One morning as we ate, Jim reached for his coffee cup and could not find the handle. Another time he fumbled with the spoon as if it were moving away from his groping fingers. Then he became unable to open the little jelly packets. Over the course of about a year, he went from eating independently to needing help with everything from buttering his toast to putting the cream in his coffee. I even had to cut up his eggs and pancakes in order for him to manage them.

During this same time period, Dave—the head custodian and Jim's boss—also began to see signs of decline. Jobs that had always been finished flawlessly were now left partially completed. One day, on his daily mail run, he left his keys and a stack of mail lying at the post office. Inexplicably, he began to forget how to perform tasks he had been doing for years. Dave simplified tasks when he could, though Jim insisted on continuing to do the same jobs as before. Dave talked to Dad, and they agreed to have Jim work a shortened day, arriving and leaving on the bus with the elementary kids, rather than with the high schoolers. His new schedule allowed him to continue serving the kids who participated in the breakfast program and perform a simplified version of his morning routine. He needed more prompting and prodding to get tasks done, and showed more inclination to argue, instead of respecting authority figures as he had in the past.

Apparently, in Jim's mind, the job description remained the same as it had always been, making Dave's supervision of him more difficult when he saw Jim attempting things that put him at risk of endangering himself. For instance, he could no longer safely set up the lunch tables, but it had always been his job, and he wasn't about to give it up.

This dilemma soon led to another shortening of Jim's work day, as Dave, Dad and the principal met and agreed that Dad should bring Jim to work after lunch, so Dave could have the tables put away before Jim got there. That took care of the lunch table problem, but soon it was evident that even the simplified chores were more than Jim could manage.

In the spring of 1998, with deep regret, my parents filled out the papers for his retirement. One of the benefits offered was long term care insurance. They couldn't imagine a situation in which Jim would be in need of long-term care, but the cost was minimal, so they signed him up. They were soon to view this as a sure sign of the Lord's guidance.

Retirement to most people means a time of relaxation and well-earned rest after a lifetime of toil. Jim, not being most people, was incensed by the thought that his job was to be taken away, and refused to even discuss it. Dad, knowing the depth of Jim's love for the job, yet realizing his regression made continued employment impossible, arranged with Dave to let Jim come in for an hour or so several times per week on a volunteer basis during the next school year. Indeed, all the folks at Chapman School assured Dad that they would be happy to have Jim there as often as he was able.

That spring, we drove to Soldotna and attended the ceremony the school district held for the year's retirees. We carefully avoided the word "retirement," knowing that Jim flatly refused to entertain such an idea. He accepted his parting gift from the superintendent: a gold pan, engraved with his name and dates of employment, which the district gives to each retiree. He posed for pictures, enjoyed the buffet meal, and received handshakes and congratulations. I believe he thought the gathering was simply in acknowledgment of his work, which he fully intended to continue as long as the breath of life was in him.

Then some well-meaning person spilled the beans. Shaking Jim's hand, the man said, "Well, Jim, what will you do, now that you're retired?" The only word Jim heard was the last one. "No!" he exclaimed vehemently. "I'm not gonna lose my job." His understanding of retirement was that it was a shameful thing. It meant he had lost his job; worse yet, he had lost it because someone was unhappy with his work.

At another of our Saturday breakfasts, shortly after the retirement ceremony, I broached the subject, thinking maybe I could put a positive spin on it. I told him, "Jim, you worked hard and now you get to rest."

His response was typical Jim: "I don't wanna lose my job. I work hard...I do a good job. I love my job. They can't take my job."

I tried to reassure him by saying that he had done such a good job that he got to stop working. I might as well have saved my breath. He kept repeating, "I wanna work. I don't wanna lose my job." We should all have such a love for our jobs after more than a quarter-century.

Just a few months following his retirement the Friday evening phone calls ceased. The first week it happened I called him; he said he was sick. The next week he was too busy. I finally told him he didn't need to make excuses, just tell me he didn't want to go anymore. Losing interest in something that had meant so much to him—to say nothing of breaking an established routine—baffled us.

We saw many of Jim's favorite activities begin to lose their ability to charm. In spring of 1998, following the demise of the four-wheeler, Dad replaced it with a shiny new one. It was simpler to run than its predecessor had been; in fact, it operated much like the original three-wheeled rig. Back then, Jim had learned to drive in a flash. Now, Dad was obliged to start the vehicle for him and put it in gear. Jim drove it a few times, then seemed to lose interest completely. It spent the next couple of years parked in the garage, till finally Dad turned it over to Ron's kids, who made it earn its keep.

That winter, as the family came together for traditional holiday gatherings, Jim showed little inclination to be involved. He confused the names of his brothers and nephews, and withdrew from group activities unless coaxed to join. Ron, convinced that this might be the last year Jim would be able to play pinochle, urged the family to give him every opportunity to participate, even though his playing was more erratic than ever.

At this same time I noticed an about-face in his attitude toward televised ball games. In the past he had been the one who cranked up the volume on the TV during football games, and scolded anyone who tried to talk over the racket. Now, I saw him sitting in his recliner, staring at the blank screen. I turned it on, thinking he'd enjoy a game. He snapped, "Shut that off! I hate that junk!" He glared at me till I turned it off.

A family birthday party brought further evidence of his changing mental ability. Ron's daughters, knowing the glee Jim exhibited when he found the toothpick, engineered the situation to make sure he got it. This time, however, he ate the cake without his usual excavation, and probably would have swallowed the toothpick whole if someone had not prevented him.

In the months following Jim's retirement, a number of new, uncharacteristic and rather odd behaviors cropped up. One that caused Mom considerable concern was the Battle of the Phantom Beetles. Jim began insisting there were beetles in his bed, that they were crawling on his feet. This put Mom on her mettle. Woe betide any creepy crawly with the temerity to invade her territory.

She started with a thorough wash of all Jim's bedding, including blankets and pillows. She bought all-cotton socks, and eliminated all laundry additives such as softeners and antistatic cling sheets, in case they were causing some sort of allergic reaction. He continued complaining. She dragged the mattress outside and gave it a thorough airing. It didn't help. Finally, she bought a new mattress and bedding, but the beetle problem remained.

Soon Jim claimed the beetles were in his socks. He could not sit for more than a minute or two without yanking them off. Then, grasping them by the tops, he sat and twirled them like limp cotton batons. This behavior—bizarre but tolerable in the living room—proved downright embarrassing when we would catch sight of him during church, a sock rotating like a propeller in each hand.

I observed Jim one evening as he lay in his recliner, watching "Wheel of Fortune," his stockinged feet on the extended footrest. Suddenly, his feet shot up, precisely as if he had indeed been bitten. He grappled wildly with the socks, seemingly in a panic to remove them. Once they were off, he relaxed and resumed watching his show, socks whirling on either side of his head.

The root of his complaint remained a mystery. We knew no self-respecting beetle would venture into Mom's domain, and if one had, even the hardiest specimen would soon have succumbed to her repeated assaults. We finally decided, based on his actions, that his feet were either numb or tingling, although the regular 3-year medical examinations required by his job turned up no physical ailment that would cause such a symptom. (My parents, as dyed-in-the-wool homesteaders, had stringent criteria for a trip to the medical clinic: either some body part had fallen off and would not reattach itself, something was bleeding and refused to be stanched, or one's temperature had just blown the end off the oral thermometer. Invisible beetles did not qualify as a cause to head to the doctor.)

Jim developed some new rituals that bordered on obsessions. One involved the way he tied his shoes. He learned to tie his shoes as a youngster, and for most of his life, performed the task with speed and efficiency. The first change in this area we noticed was his preoccupation with the length of the laces. They had to measure exactly the same length. Each time he tied them (which was about forty times as often as he actually needed to) he pulled the strings up, held them taut and compared lengths. If one was slightly shorter, he tugged and adjusted until they matched.

Next he began making double ties, but not in the usual way, by crossing and wrapping the loops around each other. No, he made his first bow a thing of beauty, adjusting the loops and strings until utterly symmetrical. Then, taking the two strings, he proceeded to make a second set of loops, again making sure they and the remaining strings were exactly uniform. If any part of this complicated procedure appeared lacking in absolute symmetry, he pulled a string, untied the whole thing, and started the entire process again. His quest for the perfect tie might continue for a half hour, until the product met his exacting standards. Of course, shortly after completing this elaborate task, the whole effect was ruined as some inner urge compelled him to pull the shoes off so he could again twirl the socks.

Jim's neatness gene also kicked into overdrive during this period. He always had been careful about putting trash in its proper place, but now his innate tidiness became a compelling force that would not be denied. Not content just to drop an item into the trash can, he followed up by manually cramming it down to the very bottom. Mom lined her garbage bins with paper bags, so he inevitably managed to crush the liner bags, as well. He established a circuit through the house, pausing at each trash receptacle and mashing all contents, real and imagined, till they were suitably flattened. Satisfied, he would relax until he either had occasion to throw something away, or one of the trash cans caught his attention, triggering the need to make the rounds again.

Before long, his desire for garbage apparently outgrew the amount of rubbish available, and he began collecting fantasy trash. This he faithfully lugged to the nearest can, and squashed carefully to the bottom. Sometimes he brought these offerings to one of us, as if unable to find a place to throw them away. He seemed so befuddled, we always played along and "disposed" of them for him. As invisible and unreal as they seemed to us, they definitely had substance in his mind.

His inner thermostat seemed to go haywire during this time. He rarely wore long sleeved shirts prior to this, preferring to choose from his wide selection of short-sleeved polos. Now, he was always cold. He refused, on the warmest summer day, to set foot outside without a knit cap and winter coat. When the rest of us shed our sweaters and opened windows, Jim yelled at us to shut the windows and went hunting for a warm jacket. Even swathed in extra layers, his hands remained icy to the touch.

We saw other signs that Jim was losing his physical faculties. His hearing, which had always been good, suddenly suffered a drastic drop. We often had to speak directly into his ear in order for him to hear. A visit to the eye doctor confirmed that he had virtually no sight in one eye, meaning his depth perception, too, was nonexistent.

At church, Don felt the brunt of this change, as Dad asked him not to invite Jim to assist with communion, fearing he would drop the trays or fall as he navigated the few steps off the podium. Loss of this job seemed almost as traumatic for Jim as retiring from the school. For several months, he continued to hound Don, wanting to know why he was not allowed to help. He even took to wearing the glasses he had been prescribed for close-up work, obviously figuring that glasses would demonstrate that he was as fit as ever for service. Though it nearly broke Don's heart, he knew that, for safety's sake, he had to turn him down.

When it became obvious that he could no longer safely climb the stairs to his upstairs room, my parents—with help from Ken's two strapping teenage sons—constructed a small addition off of their own bedroom. With carpet and paneling, they turned it into a snug little place. Mom hung some of Jim's Special Olympics trophies and other treasures on the walls. To keep from over-cluttering the room, she brought in a portable clothes rack for his shirts and pants, and a small cardboard dresser to house his underwear and socks. She fitted a scrap of the wood paneling to the dresser top, thereby giving him a spot for his beloved radio alarm clock.

As if to underscore the need for this change in room placement, Jim began taking some nasty falls. It seemed like each time I saw him, he had a new scrape on his head or arm.

Early one morning shortly after Jim moved into his new room, Dad heard an odd noise coming from Jim's nook. Leaping out of bed, he hurried in to see what was going on. He found Jim half-kneeling, half-sprawled with his face mashed against the top of the small cardboard dresser. Though Dad had not seen it happen, it was obvious that Jim had fallen, slamming his head down on the wooden panel on the dresser top, breaking the paneling and cutting a deep gash in the middle of his forehead.

My parents rushed him to the doctor, where they spoke first to a nurse with whom they were unfamiliar. She asked how he received such a wound. When they replied that he had fallen against a dresser, the nurse seemed skeptical, apparently not seeing that particular wound as consistent with falling against a dresser. To their shock, they were then questioned closely by the doctor as well, obviously suspected of abusing Jim. They hardly knew how to respond, not having seen him fall, and not knowing what precipitated it. They finally left the clinic with a new appreciation for those who are falsely accused but have no way of proving their innocence.

One Sunday in the spring of 1999, I was sitting behind my mother and Jim in church (Dad was song leader again that day, so he was seated up front). During the sermon I noticed Jim's head resting on Mom's shoulder. This was highly unusual, as he was always attentive during services. Soon it was obvious that he was unconscious; his whole weight sagged against Mom. She nudged him, and he sat up as if nothing had happened; then, within minutes, it happened again. This time we who were sitting nearby reached out to help, then he again sat up on his own. We decided to have him go sit in the nursery where there was an armchair. I helped Mom and Jim's teacher friend, Donna Austin, walk him out of the auditorium and we settled him in the chair. Although he wanted to go back and join the service, we made him stay put.

Donna's husband, RJ—an emergency medical technician— was having trouble staying awake through the church service. He'd had a late run on the ambulance the night before, and now struggled against the effects of too little sleep and a too-comfortable pew. Just as he was about to succumb, he heard a soft whisper, "RJ!" His eyes popped open and he hazily thought, "Uh-oh, the Lord is coming for me. I'm gonna die right here in church." The call came again, sounding closer and more urgent, "*RJ!*" A hand clamped onto his shoulder. He swung around to behold, not the beckoning hand of Death, but the worried face of his wife. She led him to the nursery, where he checked Jim's pulse and blood pressure, both of which registered normal.

As the service came to a close, Dad became aware of Jim's difficulties, and he immediately hustled back to the nursery to see what was going on. Jim wanted to go socialize and he seemed to feel okay, so they let him get up and leave the nursery.

A few minutes later as he shook hands and visited, with no warning, he dropped to the floor. By the time we family members realized what happened, he was struggling to get up while several people tried to convince him to stay lying down until RJ could get to him. Once again, all his vital signs were normal and he was determined to be on his feet. Jim was difficult to dissuade when he got his mind set on anything.

Several of the men helped get him out to the car; he seemed to be over whatever had ailed him, so we went to a nearby restaurant for lunch. (Jim would have been aghast if we had tried to head home without going out to eat. "Sunday dinner out" was one routine that he still looked forward to each week.)

As we took our seats at the table, I noticed that he seemed very pale, and resolved to keep an eye on him. I would have done better to keep a hand on him; we were barely seated when he fell out of his chair, hitting the floor with a loud thump. This time when the EMTs arrived, they didn't have to try too hard to convince my parents to let them take him to the hospital in Homer.

Though his vital signs showed no problems, the doctor decided to keep him overnight for observation. He was fine through the night, and they were on the verge of releasing him in the morning when, without warning, his heart stopped. If he had not been in the hospital, he may not have revived from that episode.

The doctor decided Jim needed to have a pacemaker implanted, a procedure which had to be done in Anchorage, so off he flew on the medical evacuation helicopter. Dad and Mom immediately started the 5-hour drive to be with him. Our brother John, and Tim's wife, Melody, met the chopper when it landed in Anchorage. Jim was beside himself, crying, yelling, fighting the restraints, pulling out the IVs. No words would soothe him. It took everyone there to hold him and prevent him from injuring himself or someone else.

This sort of behavior was so out of character for Jim that the family hardly knew how to deal with it. In retrospect, we wonder if perhaps he was reacting to one of the medications that he was being given for pain. The doctors in Anchorage implanted a pacemaker which regulated his heartbeat, and in a week he returned home.

From that point, we saw Jim decline steadily. It was as if he became an old man right before our eyes. He could not walk more than a few feet unassisted, and would often fall when he tried to get out of a chair. Dad began looping a rope around him like a seat belt when he was sitting, so he wouldn't get up and try to walk without someone to help him.

Early one morning in March of 2000, as Dad lay in bed half awake, he again heard an ominous thump in Jim's room. This time Jim lay twitching on the floor beside his bed, face pressed into the carpeting, his breathing audibly labored. Once again, the ambulance carried him into Homer to the emergency room. There the doctor examined him, suspecting that he had had a seizure, but deciding to keep him overnight for observation. On the way to his hospital bed, he fell backwards in a grand mal seizure.

The seizure itself lasted several minutes; when it ended the staff got him into bed. He remained uncommunicative for another thirty minutes or so, then was distressed and disoriented for several more hours. I was glad that my parents' first witness to the whole process happened at the hospital, where they could observe the staff's response and get practical advice on their role.

With the confirmation of the doctor's suspicion, they were told that there was no reason to rush in to the hospital each time Jim had a seizure, as long as they made sure he was safe. They took him home, and prepared the house and themselves as best they could to meet Jim's changing physical and medical needs. They got a wheelchair to move him around safely. Medication helped cut down on the frequency and severity of seizures. When they realized that he often had a seizure when getting out of bed in the morning, they bought a hospital bed with side rails to keep him corralled until they could help him up.

The rate of Jim's decline seemed to accelerate even more. Seizures became a common occurrence, though he had never experienced any in his entire life. The fall onto the dresser top and other mysterious tumbles that had plagued him over the past year now made sense, as my parents realized he had been having small seizures. The doctor, now that he understood the reason for Jim's falls and resultant injuries, was honest and direct with my parents: Jim was suffering from Alzheimer's disease, and it was progressing at a rapid rate. He explained that a strong link has been discovered between Down's syndrome and Alzheimer's, and many older people with the syndrome will experience the same thing Jim was going through.

He also began having hallucinations. He petted animals that weren't there, picked up and disposed of dumpster loads of fantasy trash, wept and laughed for no apparent reason, and fought off and yelled at unseen persecutors. He used his slippers as basketballs and bowling balls; we never knew when a slipper might come hurtling past our heads or knees, followed by a mighty cheer.

Like so many of the experiences we had been through with Jim throughout his life, we found little information concerning precedents. Jim was the only person we knew with Down's syndrome who had reached middle age. My research on the Internet confirmed the doctor's prognosis, leading me to wonder why we had never heard of the link between Down's syndrome and Alzheimer's before.

Just as they had accepted and dealt with his condition during his early years, my parents now shouldered the responsibility of Jim's care in a typically matter-of-fact way. Sure, they were eighty years old and then some—so what? Their health was good, Jim's was not. Bring someone else in to take care of him? Why? Who wanted strangers underfoot when his parents knew his routines and idiosyncrasies better than anyone? And long-term care? Totally out of the question; why spend that kind of money when he could get all the care he needed at home?

Final Year

This next section has been the most difficult to write, as it deals with Jim's final year. It was an unsettled time, filled with unexpected changes and decisions that had to be made. As I thought back to this period, during which we witnessed Jim's continued downward progression, I asked the Lord, what lessons were in this for us? In Romans we are told that all things work together for good for those who love God. I knew there had to be some good in this process, somewhere.

After much prayer, I realized that the answer had been spelled out centuries ago, in the book of Ecclesiastes. For each of us there will be "a time to be born, a time to die." However we react to that statement, it remains a fact. We have no say in the matter. What we do control is choosing how we will spend the time between those two events. Watching Jim's decline was a heart wrenching experience, but it in no way devalued his life and accomplishments. We all will eventually reach the end of our time on this earth, as Jim did; let us use our time wisely, appreciating the life and abilities we have, and give our best while we are able.

In June of 2000, I knock on my parents' front door and walk in. I'm greeted by the sight of a pajama-clad Jim, sitting in his wheelchair at the table. He wears a towel tied on like a bib, while Dad feeds him breakfast. I go over, put my hand on his shoulder, and speak loudly, "Good morning, Jim!" His face slowly turns toward my voice, but his expression remains blank, showing no recognition of me.

Jim now spends all his waking hours either in the wheelchair or in his recliner. I think back to last year, when we celebrated his 54th birthday at one of his favorite Homer eateries. At that time he walked into the restaurant—with my parents each holding one of his hands—ate a meal with some assistance to manipulate his spoon, and even conversed with the assembled family members, though he was a little confused as to who was whom. Now, he doesn't even know me, whom he sees almost daily; some days he doesn't seem to recognize Mom and Dad.

A month or so earlier, the process of hoisting him in and out of the car became so arduous that my parents quit taking him out, which meant that they could no longer leave the house together. They've adapted, with Dad doing post office runs and other errands, while Mom stays home with Jim. In order for them both to attend church services, they take turns, one of them staying with him on Sunday morning, the other in the evening.

He is unable to use the regular bathroom. When breakfast is over, Dad wheels him into his bedroom, and I help hoist him onto the "pot," yet another of Dad's necessity-driven creations. Its design is quite ingenious. Constructed of plywood, it looks like a big kitchen chair with a hole in the seat. Sturdy arms prevent Jim from falling. Mom has padded the arms with soft cloth to keep him comfortable. A stainless steel shelf under the seat holds a basin, which can be removed from the rear. This opening also provides access to take care of his personal cleanliness needs.

Some days he is able, with Mom and Dad steering him by the arms, to support his own weight long enough to stand, pivot and seat himself on the pot. Other days he lacks the muscle control for even that simple task, and he's a dead weight.

I worry about my parents' health; Dad is 86, and Mom is 80. They're on-call 24 hours a day, 7 days a week. Every night they get Jim up at least once to sit on the pot. If he doesn't have success on the first attempt, they get up and try again in a few hours. If he still doesn't manage to produce, they'll be up in another hour or so, trying yet again. Many nights, in spite of their vigilance, he wets the bed. I have tried to convince them to put a diaper on him and let him rest—and get some rest themselves—but they resist. It almost seems to me that, by refusing to give in on this issue, not putting him in diapers, they're trying to deny his worsening condition.

Now, as Jim sits on the pot, Dad gives him his daily sponge bath. I help Mom put fresh sheets on his bed. When the bed is made, Mom applies medication to Jim's scalp. Through the years, he has waged a losing battle with baldness and eczema. Every school year his hair almost entirely disappeared. During the summers, a little peach fuzz would grow back. As soon as the hair appeared, so did the sores. Now he has a pretty nice crop of fuzz, and Mom conscientiously does her best to keep it eczema-free.

Next, we help get him dressed and ready for the day. His

shirt is a pullover: Mom says loudly, "Two hands!" Jim responds by lifting his arms, and we slide the shirt on. Dad slips Jim's pants over his feet, then two of us hoist him upright while the third pulls the pants up and fastens them. Inwardly I shudder, thinking of all the times these two elderly people do this task without any third-party assistance.

Once he's dressed, they decide to try to walk him to the living room. This is one of his better days, meaning he seems to be able to bear his weight a little. Dad and I each take an arm, and walk him slowly through the house to the living room. Mom follows closely with the wheelchair, ready to scoot in if Jim's legs suddenly collapse. We know the importance of activity in maintaining healthy function of everything from his lungs to his digestion, so we push him to walk whenever he is able.

He makes it to the living room without mishap, and we deposit him in the recliner. Mom arranges his pillows and blankets until she is satisfied that he is comfortably established. Dad goes back to the bedroom and cleans up the pot, readying it for its next use.

Throughout Jim's life, my folks have accepted his care as their responsibility, and despite the urging of the rest of us to get some type of assistance, they continue handling it themselves. Dad spends hours each week on his knees, sponge-bathing Jim, cleaning him up after bowel movements, performing all the intimate tasks needed to maintain his health. Mom washes multiple sets of bedding, often remaking the bed two or three times in a night when their nocturnal sessions of setting Jim on the pot prove ill-timed. The two of them work together to dress, feed, and transfer him.

On this day I am at my parents' house to provide the one bit of respite that they will allow: I will spend the day here with Jim while they drive 80 miles up the road to our nearest shopping area of any size, the "twin cities" of Kenai and Soldotna. I see them off with a sense of relief, knowing that they will have a few hours in which they can shop, go out for lunch, and just relax from the constant pressure of caring for Jim.

Once they're gone, I turn on "The Price is Right" and try to interest him in the show. He gives no indication that he's aware of it. I put a cassette with some of his favorite march tunes in the tape player and crank it up loud. No response.

He sleeps for a large portion of the day. At noon, I put him in his wheelchair while I make us a simple lunch of sandwiches, fruit and tea. Jim eats what I put into his mouth, without seeming to know what he's eating.

After lunch, he's acting sleepy again, so I put him on the pot, then help him back into his recliner, where he dozes off. Mid-afternoon, as he is beginning to awaken, he suddenly moans and stiffens as a seizure grips his body. This is one of his bigger ones, with his whole body racked by jerking and trembling. There's nothing I can do except make sure he's safe and not injuring himself. When it's over, his breathing comes raspy and labored, slowly returning to normal over the space of about a half-hour. Finally, he drifts back to sleep.

Throughout that summer, my brothers and I watched helplessly as our parents doggedly refused to give over more of Jim's care into anyone else's hands. I knew my small bit of daily help and the once-a-week day of Jim-sitting would come to an end when school resumed in the fall. Robert took a week's leave from his job as an Anchorage police officer and shouldered as much of the burden as they would allow. Tim, John and Ken, though none of them lived in the Anchor Point area, all stayed in touch by phone, and came down whenever they could to lend a hand. Ron, who lived nearby, let Mom and Dad know that he was available whenever they needed help. All they needed to do was call. The problem was getting them to make that call. Various grandkids and other relatives offered to come and stay with them in order to help out; all offers were politely but firmly refused.

We urged Mom and Dad to consider hiring someone to come in and, at least, help with lifting Jim when needed. That sounded to them like they'd be putting someone to a lot of trouble; besides, how could that person know when they needed help? They figured it'd be better if they just continued doing it themselves.

By fall, it was obvious that the burden was becoming too great for them to continue. They were exhausted from lack of sleep, and both were developing back problems from the physical stress of hoisting Jim from bed to chair to pot and back again. He had lost some weight during his illness, but he was several inches taller than Mom, and still outweighed her by more than twenty pounds. More and more frequently during transfers, his feet wouldn't cooperate and Dad and Mom bore his entire weight. Many days he seemed unable to maintain an upright position. He'd lean so far to the right or left that one of his hands dragged on the floor beside the wheelchair. Even in his recliner, he couldn't stay upright without pillows packed around him to hold him in place.

In November, the doctor sat my parents down and spoke bluntly with them. He managed to get across what we had been unable to convey: it was time for Jim to enter a care facility where he would have access to round-the-clock attention from trained providers. My parents were assured that they could see him as often as they liked. We siblings all breathed a collective sigh of relief upon hearing that they'd agreed to put him in the Homer hospital's long-term care facility.

Our parents, however, still had trouble letting go. I was the first recipient of the news, since I lived closest to them. I quickly expressed my feelings that it was high time, if for no other reason than that his care would be shared by a greater number of providers. "These people are trained for this sort of work," I asserted, "and they only have to work for a certain number of hours per day, then they get away from the job and rest up. Surely it's safer for everyone than for Jim's total care to fall on the same two people day in, day out. Besides, the place is set up for people with needs like Jim's, and has instant access to medical assistance when necessary." Though I didn't add that I feared that Jim would die at home and somehow they'd be blamed or feel they were at fault, it was in my mind.

After I'd spoken my piece, Mom asked, "What do you think the boys will say?" Meaning my brothers. She still felt that, somehow, there must be more she could and should do.

Thanks to my parents' decision to sign Jim up for long term care insurance when he retired, part of the cost of his new setting was covered by insurance. He had managed to salt away a fairly tidy sum over the years he worked, as well. Although this was not the kind of support my parents envisioned when they used to talk about saving for his retirement years, they were glad their forethought had paid off. He was able, helped by his insurance, to pay all the bills out of his own money.

December 21, 2000, was moving day for Jim. Mom packed his clothing and a few personal items. Since music sometimes seemed to soothe him, she included his tape player and some cassettes with hymns and marches. She also put in a framed collage of pictures of his favorite activities, including bowling, driving his rig, and showing off his big halibut.

Ron and my husband, Charlie, helped load him into my parents' car, and we drove into Homer. The newly expanded long term care section of the hospital had obviously been built with the comfort of its clients in mind. From the dining/lounge area clients could gaze out the windows at the mountains across Kachemak Bay. A large Christmas tree lit up the lounge, while a fireplace, television, and reading area added homey touches.

Jim would have a room to himself temporarily, until more clients moved in. He had always loved Christmas lights, so I set up a small artificial tree on his dresser, and we placed his presents under it, ready for Christmas a few days hence. Through the years, several newspaper articles had been written about Jim; we brought framed copies of these to hang on his walls along with the collage.

After doing what we could to make the place feel like home, we left with heavy hearts. Intellectually, we knew this move had to happen for the health of all concerned, but, emotionally, it still felt as if we were deserting Jim. For years my parents had proved wrong the "experts" who advised institutionalization for convenience; now, outside care was a necessity. We could only thank God that we had ready access to a facility with a caring, well-trained staff, who treated each client like a member of their own family.

We were told that Jim was restless and weepy for the first few nights after the move, upset because of the strangeness of everything. He soon settled in, though, and seemed to accept the change.

Despite his diminished abilities, he still managed to steal the hearts of the staff. One woman related to us how, on one of his first nights at the facility, she positioned his wheelchair in the lounge where he could watch the flickering lights of the big Christmas tree. As she sat next to him, listening to the strains of a familiar carol, his hand began to move as if he were directing his choir of "buddies" as he had so often in the past. Suddenly he looked over at her and said clearly, "Pretty red hair." Can any woman resist a guy who compliments her hair?

After the move, my parents' lives revolved around visits to

Jim's new home. They were now relieved of the heavy lifting and nighttime duties, but they felt no less connected to this son who had been such a big part of their lives for over fifty years. Each day, they made the half-hour drive into Homer and spent several hours sitting with Jim, feeding him lunch, doing what they could to make him comfortable, and chatting with the other residents.

Dad, on seeing the staff's attempts to help Jim use their portable toilet, brought in the "pot" he had made. Jim often was unable to sit upright in his wheelchair, and leaned heavily to one side or the other. His fingers dangled dangerously near the wheels, and once or twice had gotten caught in the spokes. From cloth remnants and elastic, Mom made wheel covers to keep his fingers out of harm's way. Both the pot and the wheel covers drew exclamations of admiration from Jim's new caregivers.

Christmas came, then New Year's, Easter, Jim's birthday and Mother's Day: we ate all holiday meals with Jim. The staff at the facility made a point of decorating for and celebrating any special day that came along, encouraging each client to have as many guests for these meals as possible. Sometimes Jim's guest list included only Mom, Dad, Charlie and me; other times some of my brothers or other out-of-town family members showed up. I was touched to see how many of our relatives came to visit Jim and show support for our family. It was not easy, seeing him in that state; he showed no recognition of anybody, and sometimes was agitated, yelling and flailing with his arms.

During the months of that winter we gained a new appreciation for the impact Jim had made on the people of our town. My parents received dozens of cards from former students, teachers, and community members whose lives had been touched by his example of living life to its fullest. One young woman told my dad that she had been impressed with Jim's work ethic and dedication to his job when she attended school in Anchor Point, and was glad that he was still there when her own children started school.

As the snow of the waning winter slowly melted away, so, too, did Jim seem to fade. More often than not, on my visits I found him in bed, either recovering from a seizure or lacking the muscle control to sit in his wheelchair, even when supported by seat belts at his chest and waist. His breathing was labored and raspy from an infection that he couldn't shake. On one of my last visits, he lay in bed, gasping from the struggle to draw each breath. It had been months since he had shown any recognition or even awareness of me, yet this time his eyes looked directly into mine, as if pleading with me to help him.

A cup of water with a straw sat on the stand beside his bed. I blocked the top of the straw with my finger. Putting the straw in his mouth, I released a half-teaspoon or so of water. He swallowed and relaxed, as the water cleared his throat slightly. I sat with him, continuing to dribble tiny drips of water into his mouth each time his breathing became restricted. Finally he drifted to sleep and I left.

When he began refusing to eat, we knew his time with us was nearing its end. The doctor suggested implanting a stomach feeding tube if he continued to reject food. My parents struggled with the dilemma: they didn't believe it was right to prolong a life by artificial means, merely for the sake of keeping a heart beating. After all, if God was calling him Home, was it up to them to say "not yet"? On the other hand, if the technology was there to keep him alive, were they playing God by refusing it? Before they could reach a decision one way or the other, Jim and his Maker took the matter into their own hands.

Moving On

Jim passed from this life on June 13, 2001. His death saddened us, but also brought relief in knowing he left all suffering behind.

We laid him to rest in the woodlot behind the house, the first resident of the small family cemetery Dad had built a year before. The simple burial, on what Jim would have termed a "pretty day," was attended mainly by family and church members.

A week later, we held a memorial service at the church building, knowing there were many who wished to pay their respects. One after another, community members, former students, teachers and friends—some who came from as far away as Anchorage—stood up and shared their favorite memories. It was uplifting to hear how this simple, humble man touched so many lives, merely by being himself. The words "inspiration" and "example" came up repeatedly. I couldn't help thinking of the dire predictions given by the experts in Jim's early years. How wrong they had been. I was especially touched when a parent of one of my students, a boy with Down's syndrome, spoke. He told how Jim's example encouraged him to dream big as he considered his own son's future.

As much as Jim disliked traveling, I think his final trip out of this vale of tears was one he made gladly, because when he reached the other end, he found himself in his favorite place: Home. I can almost hear him as he enters the pearly gates, appreciatively takes in the glorious eternal warmth and light and comments, "Pretty day."

When I think of Jim in the Great Beyond, I imagine that he's doing all the things he most enjoys. Though he's freed of the limitations that restricted him here on earth, I feel sure he's still basically the same Jim. I know, upon his arrival, he'd have heard the Lord's welcoming words: "Well done, good and faithful servant. You have been faithful in a few things; I will put you in charge of many things."

Wow! *In charge. Of many things.* God has jobs for him to do! If he had any doubts that he was in Heaven, they're gone now. In his typical straightforward way he'd assure the Lord, "I do good work."

The Bible tells us that Heaven will be a place of continual

praise. This, too, is right up Jim's alley. He'll love to round up a celestial band and lead them down the streets of gold in a joyous parade. How the Heavenly mansions must be ringing with the sounds of Jim and those legions of angels whooping, cheering and singing endless hosannas to the Lord.

So Jim's life isn't ended; it's just moved to a different location. I believe he's still doing all the things he does best—serving, loving, and praising—as ever, and *forever*, with all his heart.

Jim loved music, and particularly singing. Here, he "leads the choir" in one of the many imaginary performances that gave him joy.

What gave Jim the most satisfaction, was his job as assistant custodian at Chapman Elementary School. At right, he proudly displays his 10-year pin.

Above, Jim helps custodian Tom Window prepare the school for students in August of 1987. At right, he helps to stock the school's kitchen with food. (Photos courtesy of Homer News.)

Jim discovered a passion for bowling later in his life. He and his parents were frequent visitors to Homer's bowling alley. This picture was taken around 1994.

The regard in which Jim was held by his friends and the students at Chapman Elementary School is evidenced, above, by the many get well wishes surrounding him following his pacemaker surgery in 1999.

At left, Jim displays the gold pan awarded to him by the school district upon his retirement in 1998.

Order Form

Please send _____ copies of *Onward, Crispy Shoulders!* @ $12.95 each.

I have enclosed $_____, including $2 shipping for the first book, and $1 for each additional book.

Send to the following address (please print clearly):

Your name_____

Address_____

City/State/Zip_____

Mail this form with payment to:

Fireweed Tales
Mary Perry
P. O. Box 557-A
Anchor Point, AK 99556